SCATTERSHOT

Books by Bill Pronzini

"NAMELESS DETECTIVE" NOVELS:

SCATTERSHOT
HOODWINK
LABYRINTH
TWOSPOT (with Collin Wilcox)
BLOWBACK
UNDERCURRENT
THE VANISHED
THE SNATCH

OTHER NOVELS:

MASQUES
THE CAMBODIA FILE (with Jack Anderson)
PROSE BOWL (with Barry N. Malzberg)
NIGHT SCREAMS (with Barry N. Malzberg)
ACTS OF MERCY (with Barry N. Malzberg)
GAMES
THE RUNNING OF BEASTS (with Barry N. Malzberg)
SNOWBOUND
PANIC!
THE STALKER

SCATTERSHOT

BY BILL PRONZINI

ST. MARTIN'S PRESS
NEW YORK

This one is for Collin Wilcox

Library of Congress Cataloging in Publication Data

Pronzini, Bill.
    Scattershot: a "nameless detective" mystery.

    I. Title.
PS3566.R67S36   813'.54   81-21445
ISBN 0-312-70047-4   AACR2

ONE

The bumper sticker said: *JOGGING IS FOR JERKS.*
I stood there in my brand-new blue jogging suit, panting and dripping sweat on the sidewalk, and I thought: Amen, brother. Jogging is definitely for jerks. And horse's backsides, which was what I had been feeling like as I trotted my beer belly up and down the beach at Aquatic Park. People had kept looking at me—fishermen on the pier, kids, a bunch of black musicians, even a shopping bag lady. Big, shaggy, overweight fifty-three-year-old guy in a blue jogging suit with white piping on it, running splayfooted and puffing like a Clydesdale. That was me, the spectacle. That was the horse's backside.

Kerry, I thought, I ought to strangle you.

And where was she? Not out here on this fine Sunday morning in July, making a fool of herself in *her* blue jogging suit with the white piping on it. "I might be a little late," she'd said on the phone, "so you go ahead and start without me." Yeah. She was now forty-five minutes late, and maybe she wasn't going to show up at all. Maybe she had decided, in her infinite wisdom, that she didn't want to be seen cavorting in public with a horse's ass.

The jogging had been her idea, of course—one of her current passions. "You could stand to lose a few pounds

1

around the middle," she'd said. "And jogging is fun, you'll see."

Well, I had seen, all right, and jogging was not fun. Jogging was about the least fun thing I had ever done. Jogging was for jerks.

I kept on staring at the bumper sticker. It was on the front bumper of a 1978 Datsun, and the Datsun was parked near the Aquatic Park pier at the foot of Van Ness, and I was standing on the sidewalk in front of it feeling stupid. I did not want to turn around and go lumbering back for another lap along the beach; I did not want to give the fishermen and the black musicians and the shopping bag lady another show. I wanted to take off my blue jogging suit and stuff it into a trashcan and then go get a nice cold beer somewhere. If it wasn't for Kerry . . .

A bald guy wearing a windbreaker came up the path from the beach and went past me to the Datsun. He stopped next to the front fender, laid a possessive hand on it, and narrowed his eyes at me. "Something about my car?" he said.

"I was just admiring your bumper sticker."

"Yeah?"

"Where did you get it?"

"Why do you wanna know?"

"I want to get one for my car," I said.

"How come? You're a jogger, ain't you?"

"Not anymore. I'm taking the pledge."

The bald guy considered that. "My brother-in-law's a jogger," he said. "He's also a jerk. That's why I put the sticker on there. It annoys hell out of him and my wife both."

"Good for you."

"Yeah. I got it in a place at the Wharf. They make them up with anything you want on 'em, as long as it ain't obscene."

"Jogging is obscene enough," I said.

He nodded sagely, gave me a crooked grin, and got into his Datsun. I turned around and looked at the path to the beach. Then I went the other way, uphill past where my own car was parked to the bocce ball courts. I loved Kerry, I would do just about anything for her, but you've got to draw the line somewhere. If she wanted me to lose weight, I would go on a diet; I would even stop drinking beer. But I was damned if I would have a heart attack for her in a blue jogging suit at Aquatic Park.

All of the bocce courts were in use, as they usually were on weekends when the weather was good. Most of the players were elderly Italians from nearby North Beach, and they approached the game with a seriousness that bordered on reverence—making wagers, arguing strategy, taking their shots with studied care. Bocce, if you don't know the game, is mostly like lawn bowling and a little like shuffleboard. The courts are long and wood-sided and dirt-floored, and the balls are made of wood, and you play in teams of three or four to a side. One player rolls a tiny pivot ball from one end of the court to the other; then each player in turn rolls a larger ball, about the size of a softball, toward the pivot, the object being to get as close to it as possible without touching it. You can make your shot straight at the pivot, or you can bank it off the wooden sidewalls. Or, if you're trying to knock an opponent's ball out of the way, when all paths to the pivot are blocked, you can even hurl your ball underhand through the air. It may sound simplistic when you break it down to its basics, but there is a symmetry and tradition to bocce that makes it fascinating. My father used to play it, back when I was a kid in Noe Valley, which is how I learned to appreciate the game. Even now I would come down here once in a while, on a Saturday or Sunday, and spend hours watching the old Italians play. I had also joined in a time or two when they were shorthanded.

I went in and sat down on one of the benches facing the near court; Kerry could find me there easily enough—if she showed up—because it was visible from the street and because she knew I liked bocce. My respiration was back to normal by this time, but I was still marinating in my own sweat. So I made sure to sit in the sun; there was a breeze off the bay, a little nippy, and now that I had avoided cardiac arrest, I also wanted to avoid pneumonia.

A couple of the old men I knew nodded and said hello to me. None of them said anything about my jogging outfit or even raised an eyebrow. That was the nice thing about old-world Italians: they were always polite and never embarrassed anyone in public. The way they figured it, people in general, and probably fifty-three-year-old horse's backsides in particular, could take care of that well enough themselves.

I had been sitting there for fifteen minutes, absorbed in the match, when Kerry arrived. I saw her come in through the gate, and I felt a little fluttery sensation in the pit of my stomach; she did things like that to me. She was thirty-eight, worked for the Bates and Carpenter ad agency, and was the daughter of a pair of onetime pulp writers; I had met her, and her parents, six weeks ago during a pulp-magazine convention and a subsequent double-homicide case that had almost got me killed. She liked private eyes because her mother had written a pulp series about one, and she thought I was a pussycat. I thought she was gorgeous. Even in a twin of my blue jogging suit she was gorgeous. She had coppery hair and a generous mouth and greenish chameleon eyes that seemed to change color according to her mood. She also had a good willowy body and a smile that could melt your chocolate bar, as a fellow private cop I know in Hollywood puts it.

4

She gave me the smile as she sat down next to me, but there was a hint of reprimand in it. "So," she said, "sitting on your ample duff."

"I went jogging," I said.

"Oh?"

"Yeah. Look at me. I'm all sweaty."

"Mm. It wasn't so bad, now, was it?"

"It was awful. I'm going on a diet instead."

"Come on, exercise is good for you."

"So is sitting in the sun like a houseplant," I said. "You're an hour late, you know that?"

"I was fiddling with that damned presentation of mine." She hesitated. "And my father called."

"Again?"

"Again."

"The same old crap, I suppose?"

"Yes and no. He wanted to tell me he's going to New York for a few days on business."

"Good. Maybe he'll leave you alone."

"He's not influencing me, you know."

"Isn't he?"

"No, he isn't."

"Then why do you keep saying no?"

"I haven't said no."

"You haven't said yes, either."

"I just need more time, that's all."

"How much more time?"

"I don't know. It's a big decision. . . ."

"Sure. *Your* decision, not your father's."

"Now look, you," she said. Her tone was light, but the lightness seemed a little forced. "Nobody makes my decisions except me. And nobody exerts any influence over me.

I'm a big girl; I don't pay much attention to parental advice anymore."

"Meaning he was after you again to push me under a bus."

"Oh God," she said. "He doesn't hate you; he's just leery of the business you're in."

"Yeah. Leery."

A shout went up from some of the bocce players: one of them had whacked an opponent's ball with an underhand air shot. I glanced over at them. When I looked back at Kerry she was staring straight ahead and her face had a cloudy, introspective cast. The set of her mouth showed a leaning toward anger.

I knew I was pushing it too much, but I could not seem to help myself. I loved her, and I wanted her so damn badly it was becoming an obsession. The first time I had asked her to marry me, we'd been sitting on the balcony of her Diamond Heights apartment; it had been just after the end of the pulp convention case and I had known her four days. She'd been surprised, flattered—and reticent. She liked me, she said, and maybe she loved me too, but she wanted to be absolutely sure; she had been through one bad marriage, to a schmuck L.A. lawyer named Ray Dunston, and she just wasn't sure if she wanted to try it again. Okay, I said, so we'll live together first, what about that? Maybe, she said. Give me some time to think it over.

So I gave her some time; I didn't mention marriage or a living arrangement for the next couple of weeks. We went out together, we slept together, we spent good quiet evenings at her apartment and at my Pacific Heights flat. And I thought she was weakening, from things she said, little hints she dropped, and I got ready to bring up the subject again. But then her father called, and she made the mistake of telling him about my proposal, and that was when Ivan the

Terrible started his long-distance telephone campaign. With the result that when I did restate my proposal, Kerry put me off. And had been putting me off ever since.

Ivan Wade didn't like me worth a damn. He thought I was too old for Kerry; he thought I was a fat, scruffy private detective and had told me so to my face during the pulp convention. He was a stuffy, overprotective, humorless old fart, Ivan was. He had seen his daughter through one messy relationship; he did not want to see her through another, which was what he was convinced would happen if she hooked up with me. He was after her all the time about the perils and insecurities of my job, about the difference in our ages, about Christ knew what else that she wasn't telling me. And he was beginning to wear thin on me. If he didn't cut it out pretty soon I was inclined to fly down to Los Angeles and confront him about it. Kerry wouldn't like that, but it seemed to be my only course of action. As it was, I had tried to reason with him through her, which had proved futile. I had even called Kerry's mother, Cybil, who pretty much approved of me—maybe because I had uncovered and then reburied some skeletons in her closet during the double-homicide thing, or maybe just because she liked me—but that had not done any good, either. Cybil was a forceful personality, but when it came to Ivan the Terrible she seemed more often than not to come off second best.

Kerry had her hands folded on one knee; I put my hand on her laced fingers. "Hey," I said, "I'm sorry. I didn't mean to come on so strong."

"No, it's all right," she said. But she didn't smile.

"It's just that I love you."

"I know."

"So make your decision soon, huh?"

"Yes. Soon."

I looked at her for a time. "Crazy," I said.

"What's crazy?"

"Me. I feel like a kid when I'm around you."

"You are a kid sometimes. Big, tough private eye. Hah."

"Hah," I agreed.

She reached over and straightened the damp collar of my jogging-suit top, and this time I got a smile. "Big, sloppy, persistent kid," she said. "All right, kid, let's go jogging."

"Uh-uh. I've had enough of that."

"No, you haven't. You need the exercise."

"There are other forms of exercise."

"Like what?"

I told her like what.

She said, "It's not even noon yet."

"So?"

"So didn't you have enough Friday night?"

"Sure. But this is Sunday."

"We can do that later, you sex fiend. Right now I want to go jogging, and then I want to go to your flat and take a shower, and then I want to have some lunch."

"Jogging first?"

"Jogging first. Come on."

Jogging is for jerks, I thought. But I let her prod me up and lead me out of the bocce courts and down toward the beach. Then, by God, I let her start me running and puffing and dripping sweat again, while the fishermen and a bunch of tourists and the black musicians gawked at the sight.

The ordeal lasted an hour. I didn't have a heart attack, but I was hurting plenty as I drove, with Kerry following in her car, down Van Ness and up to my flat. She got into the shower first, which gave me time to guzzle two cans of Schlitz; I'll start my diet tomorrow, I thought, the hell with it. Then I took my shower and let the hot water work out some of the muscle knots. Then we had lunch. Then we went to bed.

And for the first time between us, it wasn't all that good. Kerry knew it too; we didn't say much to each other afterward. I asked her to have dinner out somewhere, stay the night, but she said no, she wanted to do some more work on her agency presentation. She left at five-thirty, and when she was gone the flat felt empty and I felt empty. I spent the evening reading one of her mother's Samuel Leatherman private eye novellas in a 1946 issue of *Dime Detective*—one of the sixty-five hundred pulp magazines I collect and keep on bookshelves in the living room. That wasn't very good, either. At eleven I went to bed and lay there listening to the silence and to the mutterings inside my head.

I'm going to lose her, I thought.

Jogging, diets, proposals, love—none of that would make any difference. Ivan the Terrible was going to get his way. Damn it, I was going to *lose* her.

TWO

Blue Monday.

I was in a funk when I got down to my new offices at nine-twenty—a pale blue funk, two shades lighter than dark blue depression. The place did nothing to buoy up my spirits. It was on Drumm Street, within pitching distance of the Hyatt Regency and the moribund Embarcadero Freeway, and I had been occupying it just about as long as I had known Kerry. The building was newly renovated and the elevators did not clank as they went up and down; the anteroom and the private inner office had chrome chairs with corduroy cushions and venetian blinds on the windows; the walls were pastel-colored, the carpet was beige, the telephone was yellow, and the fact that I was blue made it a Technicolor nightmare.

No character, that was the problem with it. My old office, on the fringe of the Tenderloin, where I'd spent twenty years of my life, had been dripping with character: scarred walls, battered furniture, sagging rail dividers, a gloomy alcove with a sink in it that had been old in the days of Sam Spade. That, by God, had been a private eye's office. This was the office of a salesman or a lawyer or a minor business executive: pleasant, unobtrusive, and sterile. It wasn't *mine.* Not even the blowup poster of a *Black Mask* cover I had hung on one wall made it mine.

I kept telling myself that when I got used to it I would feel more at home here; that given enough time, I could mark it with my individual stamp. But I didn't believe it. I wished I was back on Taylor Street, in my crumbling old digs, and the hell with what clients and prospective clients thought, the hell with image and being upwardly mobile. I was fifty-three, I had been a private cop for better than two decades, I had made a decent living. What did I want to start changing my life for?

Rhetorical question. Here I was, in my bright, shiny new offices. And here I was, mooning around like a lovesick teenager, all but begging a woman fifteen years my junior to become my wife. I had been a bachelor for fifty-three years, too, and what did I want to change *that* part of my life for?

Damn, I thought. Damn.

I sat down at my desk and looked out through the venetian blinds I had just opened. It was a decent day, sunny, a little haze, and I could see some of the activity at the piers along the Embarcadero. The faint moan of a ship's horn, probably the one on the Sausalito ferry, penetrated the office silence. I sat like that for a time, looking out, thinking too much. Then I got up and put some water on the hot plate for coffee.

In my old office I had kept the hot plate on top of my single file cabinet; here I had a separate little table for it, with jars of instant coffee and dairy creamer and sugar and a package of plastic spoons and another package of styrofoam cups all laid out next to it. Maybe I ought to bring in a tray of doughnuts and cake every morning, I thought; give my clients a real treat. Or, hell, bring in another hot plate and a pasta machine and some marinara sauce, whip up some spaghetti, give them a real Italian meal to go with their real Italian private eye—

The telephone rang.

I had already checked and shut off my answering machine —no weekend messages. So I went over and hauled up the receiver on the pimp-yellow phone and said, "Detective agency," in my pale blue voice.

A prim, rather stuffy male voice asked me who was speaking. I told him, and he said, "You're a detective?" and I thought: No, I'm a horse's ass. But I said, "Yes, that's right. May I help you?"

"My name is George Hickox. I represent Mr. Clyde Mollenhauer."

The inflection he put on the second name said that I was supposed to recognize it. But I had never heard of anyone named Clyde Mollenhauer. Or, for that matter, anyone named George Hickox.

"Yes?"

"Mr. Mollenhauer has need of a private security guard. Do you do that sort of work?"

"I have in the past, yes."

"Would you be available this coming Saturday?"

"For how many days?"

"Just Saturday."

"Let me check my calendar," I said. My calendar was as sterile as the office, but you never want to sound too eager. I sat holding the phone for fifteen seconds; then I said, "Saturday looks free, yes. What sort of security service are we talking about, Mr. Hickox?"

"I'd prefer to discuss that in person, if you don't mind. I could stop by for an interview later this afternoon."

Interview. My, my. "That would be fine. What time would be convenient for you?"

"Three o'clock."

"I'll expect you then."

"Yes," he said and hung up without adding a good-bye.

The telephone rang again twenty minutes later, while I was drinking coffee and preparing invoices and strongly worded letters for a couple of deadbeat clients. You get a few like that—people who hire you and then decide that the work you did was unsatisfactory, or who just don't like to part with their money. The amounts owed me on these two cases were less than two hundred dollars each, but the debts had been outstanding for months. Either they paid up immediately or I would have to take them to small-claims court; that was what I told each of them in my strongly worded letters.

This call was from an attorney named Adam Brister, whom I did not know. He said he had got my name from another lawyer, one I did know and had done some work for in the past, and could I come by his office in an hour to discuss a small investigative matter. I said I could, took down his address, and thanked him for calling me. I didn't bother to ask him what sort of investigative matter he had in mind; a lot of my business comes from attorneys—small

12

stuff, mostly, bread-and-butter cases—and when one of them contracted me I pretty much knew what to expect.

The job Adam Brister had for me turned out to be typical enough. His office was on Clement Street, out near the park, and he was young, brisk, businesslike, and greedy-eyed. He sat me down in his client's chair and laid a glossy color photograph of a woman in front of me. While I was looking at the photo he got straight to the point.

"The woman is Lauren Speers," he said. "Do you know the name?"

"I'm afraid not."

"Well, she's a local socialite—worth several hundred thousand dollars, all inherited money. She has quite a few important friends—politicians, actors, capitalists—and she travels constantly. The jet-set type. Very hard to locate unless she wants to be located. I'm sure you know what I mean."

I nodded. The woman in the photograph had striking red hair and green eyes and was beautiful enough if you liked them forty and dissipated. Booze or drugs, or maybe just her jet-set life-style, had taken a pretty stiff toll; in another few years she would be fat and blowsy, and her beauty would be nothing but a memory.

"She is also a reckless person," Brister said, "especially when she's been drinking. She drives a Porsche and she's had several accidents; the only reason she's kept her license is that she has those influential friends."

I nodded again and gave him back the photograph.

"A few weeks ago," he said, "she sideswiped a car belonging to a client of mine, Vernon Inge. Hit-and-run. Mr. Inge got her license number and reported the incident to the police, but of course they haven't done much. Speers has dropped out of sight; no one knows, or owns up to knowing, where she is."

I knew what was coming, now. "Your client is bringing a damage suit against her, is that right?"

"Yes. He suffered a severe whiplash as a result of the accident, and he has been unable to work since. The papers have all been filed and a court date arranged; it's a simple matter of finding Speers and serving her with a subpoena. That is where you come in."

Uh-huh. And so much for the glamorous role of the private detective in modern society. No rich client, no smoky-hot liaison with a beautiful woman, no fat fee. Just a skinny standard fee to track down a woman who apparently moved around more than the governor, hand her some papers, listen to abusive language—they always throw abusive language at you—and then exeunt and on to the next skinny standard fee. Well, that was all right. Better a job like this than no job at all. The state of my finances being what they were, I was in no position to be picky.

Brister leaned forward and studied me with his greedy eyes. One long look at those eyes told me that Vernon Inge's damage suit was a whopper; if Brister had anything to say about it, Lauren Speers was going to pay through the nose for her latest peccadillo.

He said, "Do we have an arrangement?"

"We do. Have you got a file on Speers?"

"Yes. It's fairly extensive. Names and addresses of relatives and friends, everything you should need."

"Suppose I find out she's in Switzerland or South America. Do I go after her to serve the papers?"

"I'd have to discuss that with my client," Brister said. "Let's not worry about that bridge until we come to it."

We settled on my skinny standard fee. After which I asked him a few more questions, signed a contract form he'd prepared, collected his file on Lauren Speers and a retainer check, and let him show me out. His hand was moist when he shook mine; greed does that to some people. I scrubbed away the feel of him on my pantleg as I walked to my car.

It was noon by the time I got back to Drumm Street. Some of my funk was gone; I had my mind on business, instead of on Kerry, and things seemed a little brighter than they had earlier. I stopped at a café near my building, ate a pastrami sandwich, and then went to the office to earn my fee.

I spent fifteen minutes going over the Speers file. In addition to the names and addresses of relatives and friends, there were some newspaper clippings chronicling various activities: social stuff, parties she'd attended or given, a fund raising for a local congressman; accounts of her two divorces, one from a doctor named Colwell and the other from a businessman named Eason; a recent gossip column squib linking her romantically with a well-known Hollywood TV actor; an article dealing with an arrest for drunk driving a couple of years back, which had been newsworthy because she'd led two police cars a merry chase through the Marina. None of that told me much, except to confirm what Brister had led me to believe about her.

I dragged the phone over and dialed the number listed in the file for her home address, an exclusive section of Pacific Heights. A woman's voice answered by saying, "The Speers residence." I asked for Lauren Speers, and the woman said she was sorry, Ms. Speers was out of town, and I said I was calling for the well-known Hollywood TV actor mentioned in the gossip column squib, who was anxious to talk to Ms. Speers on a matter of urgent importance. Could she please tell me where Ms. Speers might be reached? She could not. She said she would pass along the message if Ms. Speers called or returned home; then she asked, a little coldly, for my name and number. At which point I thanked her for her time and hung up on her. So much for trying to be clever.

I called a guy I knew who worked for the *Examiner*, and

through him I got to talk to the woman who edited the society page. I didn't tell her I was a detective, which would have aroused her curiosity and got me nowhere; instead I said I was a writer who wanted to interview Speers. But I got nowhere with that, either. The society editor had no idea where Speers was, nor did she know of any upcoming special events in or out of the city which Speers might be expected to attend. All I learned from her was that Speers was reputed to be writing a book, about what no one seemed to know; she offered the opinion that maybe the book was the reason why the lady had dropped out of sight.

Using various cover stories, I made half a dozen more calls to Ms. Speers's friends and relatives. The results were the same; if any of them knew where she was, they weren't talking under any circumstances. I decided I needed a different approach and went back and reread Brister's file, looking for an angle that I could pursue. I was still looking when George Hickox showed up for his three o'clock appointment.

He came in right on time; he was the type who would always be punctual. He was in his mid-thirties, brawny, heavy-featured, with styled black hair and a neat mustache, and he had a stiff-backed, vaguely supercilious air about him. His clothing was immaculate: dark three-piece suit, crisp white shirt with monogrammed cuff links, crisp blue tie with a monogrammed clip. The suit was of good quality, but it was not particularly expensive; the same was true of the cuff links and the tie clip and his polished black loafers. He may have represented money in the person of Mr. Clyde Mollenhauer, whoever *he* was, but he was not exactly wallowing in it himself.

I ushered him into the inner office and watched him look around before he took one of the clients' chairs. His lip seemed to want to curl a little when he laid eyes on the *Black*

Mask poster, but he managed to control the impulse. He sat
stiff-backed, as I knew he would, and crossed one leg over
the other and studied me the way he had the office. I must
have passed inspection, because after a moment he nodded
once and said, "What do you charge for your services?"

"That depends on what the service entails. I generally get
two hundred dollars a day, plus expenses."

"That would be satisfactory."

"Just what is it your Mr. Mollenhauer wants guarded? Or
should I say who?"

"No, it's what. Wedding presents."

"Pardon?"

"Wedding presents," Hickox said again. "Mr. Mollenhauer's daughter is being married on Saturday; the reception
will be held on his estate in Ross."

Ross, I thought. Well, now. Ross was a little Marin
County community a half-hour's drive across the Golden
Gate Bridge; it was also the kind of place that catered to
people with a lot of anachronistic ideas about class and racial
distinctions. They had a committee which screened appli-
cants for pieces of their exorbitantly priced real estate. You
could be as rich as King Midas, but if you did not measure
up to certain rigid standards, or if you happened to be a
member of a variety of ethnic groups, you would be hard-
pressed to buy your way in.

Not that everybody who lived in Ross was a bigot or a
snob, of course; most of the people were all right and had
gravitated there for the prestige, the scenery, and the best
police protection in the county. But the ones who controlled
Ross were of a type, and the types they wanted to live with
were their own. I wondered if Mr. Clyde Mollenhauer was
one of those controlling forces. If he was, I was not going to
enjoy working for him.

Hickox said, "The gifts are to be delivered prior to the

17

church ceremony, by their respective givers. Mr. Mollenhauer anticipates a number of very expensive items among them."

"I see."

"Your job will be to keep watch on them while everyone is away at the church and during the party afterward. You'll be on duty from two o'clock until eight, when the bride and groom begin opening the presents."

"That's fine."

"Do you carry a firearm?"

"No. You want me to come armed?"

"Mr. Mollenhauer would prefer it."

"Why? He's not expecting trouble, is he?"

"Of course not. It's merely an added precaution."

"All right. Whatever Mr. Mollenhauer wants."

"Yes," Hickox said, "exactly."

"Is there anything else I should know?"

"I believe that's everything."

"Okay, then. It sounds simple enough."

"It should be, yes. Do you know Ross at all?"

"I'm afraid not."

"Mr. Mollenhauer's estate is on Crestlawn Drive. Number eighty." He went on to tell me how to get there, and I dutifully wrote down the directions on my notepad. "You're to arrive by two o'clock," he said. "Please be on time."

"I will be."

He nodded. "You'll be paid at the end of your tour of duty. I trust that's satisfactory."

I said that it was. I got out one of the standard contract forms I use, filled it in, and asked Hickox to sign it as Clyde Mollenhauer's agent. He did that, but not until he had read it over at least twice.

He stood up after he handed it back to me; I stood up with him. "Do you mind if I ask you a question, Mr. Hickox?"

"Yes?"

"Just who is Clyde Mollenhauer?"

He looked surprised. "You don't know?"

"The name isn't familiar, no."

"Mr. Mollenhauer," he said stiffly, "is one of the most important men in the computer industry. He owns several companies and several patents. He is also a leading figure in political circles."

Good for him, I thought. And I'll bet I know which side of the political fence he's on, too. "It must be interesting," I said, "working for a man like that."

"Yes, it is. Very."

"What is it you do for him, if you don't mind my asking?"

He did mind my asking; his eyes said that. They also said that I was a little too inquisitive for my own good and that I would be wise if I remembered my place, whatever he thought that might be. "I am Mr. Mollenhauer's personal secretary," he said. And two seconds after that he said, "Good afternoon," and took himself out of there without bothering to shake my hand.

"Nerts to you, big boy," I said aloud. Then I sat down again and thought that it didn't matter whether I liked Hickox or his employer; what did matter was that I liked two hundred dollars a day, plus expenses, for what sounded like a nice easy job. The odds were long against any unsavory types getting wind of a cache of wedding presents and trying to rip them off. So I could just sit on my ample duff, as Kerry had put it yesterday, and indulge Mr. Clyde Mollenhauer's precautionary whim and make myself a nice fee for not much effort at all.

Jobs like that, and like the one Adam Brister had given me earlier, were not going to make me rich. But then, who wanted to be rich? Not me. Being rich meant owning an estate in Ross and hiring pompous male secretaries and worrying about thieves; being rich meant drinking too much and driving recklessly in an expensive Porsche and getting sued by greedy-eyed lawyers.

Clyde Mollenhauer and Lauren Speers could have their lives, and welcome. Me, I liked being a poor private investigator with sixty-five hundred pulp magazines, a yen for a pretty lady, and a penchant for blue funks. I liked my life just fine, thank you, the way it was.

THREE

I spent another hour with the Speers file and the telephone, without much success. I did find reference in one of the recent social clippings to Speers having hired a personal secretary, one Bernice Dolan—lots of personal secretaries running around these days, I thought—and then discovered that there was no address or telephone number for anyone of that name in the file. So I checked the White Pages and found a listing for a Bernice Dolan in Cow Hollow, not far from Speers's Pacific Heights residence. But when I called the number there was no answer. Three other calls to people on the list also drew blanks.

The file offered a couple of other possibilities, but they would require legwork. Finding La Speers was not going to be quite as simple as I'd hoped; at least, it didn't look as though I could accomplish the task by sitting on my ample duff with the telephone. It was too late to start knocking on doors today, I decided. That was for tomorrow's agenda.

At four-thirty I put the file away and dialed the Bates and Carpenter number. Fifteen seconds and one secretary later, Kerry's voice said, "Hi," in my ear.

"Hi. What's new and exciting?"

"Nothing much."

"Did you finish your presentation?"

"Yep. Last night, late."

"And they loved it, right?"

"Wrong. They want me to redo it."

"How come?"

"Problems with the concept, I'm told."

"Sounds like a rough day."

"You can say that again."

"Sounds like a rough day."

"Cute. Did anyone ever tell you you're cute?"

"You did, grumpy."

"Grumpy, yourself. How was *your* day?"

"Not bad. Two new clients."

"That's good. Beautiful rich ladies, no doubt."

"One beautiful rich lady," I said. "But I didn't get to ogle her. She's missing, and I've got to find her and serve her with a subpoena. She's being sued because she likes to play reckless games with her Porsche."

"Who's the other client?"

"A guy named Clyde Mollenhauer. He has an estate in Ross."

"Mollenhauer? No kidding?"

"You know him?"

"Sure. A VIP. Why does he want a private eye?"

"No big deal," I said. "His daughter's getting married on Saturday and I get to guard the wedding gifts."

"You're coming up in the world, my friend. Hobnobbing with the rich and the famous."

"Uh-huh. Listen, I could use a beer, and I'll bet you could use something even stronger. Why don't I meet you at the Hyatt? Then we'll go have dinner—"

"I can't," she said.

"How come?"

"Jim Carpenter is taking me to dinner tonight. He wants to talk about the presentation."

"Going out with the boss, huh? Is he the good-looking one?"

"Yes. Are you jealous?"

"Hell, no," I lied. "I'd just like to see you, that's all."

"Maybe tomorrow night. I'll have to call you."

"I'll probably be in and out all day. If I'm not here, just leave a message."

We said a few more things to each other, and then she said she had to go, and that was that. When I cradled the receiver I could feel shades of blue seeping in on me again. I felt rejected, which was probably dumb; she had a career, she had responsibilities and priorities, there was nothing wrong with her going out to dinner with one of her bosses. And yet I still sensed a distance opening up between us. I just could not shake the feeling that I was losing her.

I walked over to a place on California and drank two bottles of beer. The prospect of food didn't appeal to me; neither did the prospect of going home to my empty flat. I bought a copy of the *Examiner* and checked the movie listings. There were two classic private eye films showing at the Richelieu—*Murder, My Sweet* with Dick Powell as Philip Marlowe and *Out of the Past* with Robert Mitchum. So I collected my car and drove to Geary and took my funk into the dark theater.

I felt better when I came out four hours later, but not much. When I got home the flat smelled of dust and lingering traces of Kerry's perfume. You really are a horse's ass,

I told myself as I made a sandwich and opened another beer. Lone-wolf private dicks don't act like this. You know what Phil Marlowe would do if he walked in here right now? He'd laugh his head off, that's what he'd do. He'd fall on the floor laughing.

The hell with Phil Marlowe, I thought. I'm not Phil Marlowe; I'm me. I'm me, damn it, and I love that lady.

I went to bed. And pulled the covers over my head, like a kid alone in a big, empty house.

There was a woman waiting for me when I got down to Drumm Street on Tuesday morning.

She was hovering around the hallway, looking annoyed, and when I unlocked my office door she followed me inside. "Are you the detective?" she asked.

"Yes, ma'am, I am."

"You're supposed to be open for business at nine o'clock," she said accusingly. "That's what your ad in the telephone directory says. Do you know that it's almost nine-thirty?"

"Yes, ma'am. I'm running a little late this morning."

"I've been waiting fifteen minutes," she said. "I was just about to leave and go find someone else."

"I'm sorry if you were inconvenienced," I said, with more tact than I felt. "Is there something I can help you with?"

"Of course there's something you can help me with. Would I be here if there wasn't?" She made a sniffing noise. "My name is Edna Hornback."

She looked like an Edna Hornback. She was thin and pinch-faced, with vindictive eyes and a desiccated look about her, as if all her vital juices had dried up a long time ago. I took her to be somewhere in her mid-forties, although she had herself arranged—dyed blond hair, stylish clothes, plenty of makeup—to look ten years younger. She wore rings on eight of her ten fingers, at least a couple of which sported precious stones. Because of the obvious value of the rings, I decided I would keep on letting her be rude to me. Up to a point.

"Pleased to meet you, Mrs. Hornback," I lied. "Come into my private office. We'll talk there."

I took her through the anteroom and pointed out one of the chrome-and-corduroy clients' chairs. She sat down, put her purse on her lap, and promptly lit a cigarette. Her eyes, moving over the surroundings, showed disapproval.

"I can't say much for your decor," she said.

I didn't say anything.

"I'm an interior designer," she said. "The color scheme is all wrong; the colors clash. There's no harmony."

"I didn't design the place, Mrs. Hornback."

"Yes, well, it offends."

So do you, lady, I thought. I went over and picked up the coffeepot. "Would you care for some coffee?"

"No, thank you. I had some earlier."

I decided I didn't want any, either, and came back and sat down. "What can I do for you?"

She sighed out a lungful of smoke, straight across the desk at me. I waved it away with my hand. I used to be a two-pack-a-day man, until my doctor found a lesion on one lung; now, three years after I quit the things, cigarette smoke irritates my sinuses and makes my chest feel tight.

"I'm here about my husband," she said.

"Yes?"

"He's a miserable, no-good son of a bitch," she said, "and I'm going to fix his wagon. I am definitely going to fix his wagon."

There isn't much you can say to a statement like that. I just sat and watched her vindictive eyes and waited.

"He's got another woman," Mrs. Hornback said. "I don't suppose that surprises you."

God, no, it didn't. But I said, "Things like that happen."

"Typical male response." She made a vicious production out of jabbing her cigarette into the desk ashtray. "But that's not the worst of it. He's also a damned thief."

"Thief?"

"That's right. Over the past three years Lewis has stolen at least a hundred thousand dollars from Hornback Designs."

I frowned at her. "That's a lot of money."

"Damn right it is."

"You're partners in this design firm?"

"We *were* partners. I stupidly let him handle the books. I trusted him, the bastard."

"How did he manage to steal so much money?"

"We have a very successful business," she said; "we have a yearly income in the high five figures. It wasn't that difficult for him. He overcharged some of our customers, pocketed cash payments from others, and falsified the books. I think he also took kickbacks from suppliers."

"How did you find out about it?"

"We've had an exceptional year so far, but our bank balance doesn't reflect it. I began to suspect something funny was going on a few weeks ago. Then I found out about this bitch of his, and I *knew* something funny was going on."

"Have you confronted him?"

"Yes. He denied everything, of course. I have an auditor going over the books now, but that takes time."

"So you haven't gone to the police."

"I can't do that without proof. And I'm afraid he'll run off with the money and his bitch before I can."

"This woman—who is she?"

"I don't know," Mrs. Hornback said. "That's what I want you to find out."

"I see."

"Every day lately he leaves our office—Hornback Designs is on Union Street—every day he leaves there at five o'clock, and he doesn't come home until after midnight. It's her he goes to. I found a woman's comb in his car, cigarette butts with lipstick on them in the ashtray. That's how I know he has a bitch on the side."

A woman's comb and lipsticked cigarette butts didn't prove Lewis Hornback had a girl friend; those things could have belonged to customers or acquaintances. But I didn't tell her that. Edna Hornback was not the kind you could tell anything to, once she had her mind made up.

"I think she's the one who's keeping the money for him," Mrs. Hornback said. "I've been through his things; he doesn't seem to have an extra savings account or another safe deposit box. Or if he does, *she's* got the passbook or the key. Find her and you'll find my money. It's as simple as that."

It probably wasn't as simple as that, but I didn't tell her that, either. I said, "You want me to follow him, is that it?"

"Yes. Find out where he goes at night, who his bitch is." She paused. "What are your daily rates?"

"Two hundred, plus expenses."

She winced. And then got her face under control and drew herself up in the chair. "Well, I don't mind paying for results," she said. "And if you find my money, I'll give you a five-hundred-dollar bonus. How does that sound?"

It sounded fine, in theory. But it didn't thrill me very much. I was not convinced that Mrs. Hornback was correct in either of her allegations. Maybe old Lewis had misappropriated a hundred grand of their firm's money, but then again, maybe he hadn't; she had not given me any proof of it, nor did she seem to have any real proof of it herself. It could all be a fantasy concocted by a vengeful woman. And even if old Lewis did have another woman, as she claimed, I would be willing to bet he had justifiable cause. Not that that part of it was any of my concern. It was up to God to make moral judgments; it was up to me to make an honest living for myself.

I debated. She was not someone I cared to work for, right or wrong in her accusations. On the other hand, her money was as good as anyone else's, and if I didn't take the job she would find someone who would. I already had two clients to attend to this week, but the Mollenhauer job was not until Saturday and the Speers investigation could be handled during regular business hours. There was no real reason why I couldn't spend a few of my evenings trailing Lewis Hornback—particularly now that Kerry was spending her evenings with presentations and one of her bosses.

Mrs. Hornback was in the process of lighting another cigarette. "Well?" she said.

"All right, I'll do what I can. Do you have a photograph of your husband?"

She had one, which she fished out of a fat wallet and handed to me as if it were contaminated. Lewis Hornback was about the same age as she, with dark brown hair, a mole under his right eye, and nondescript features. He was not smiling in the photo; I had the feeling that he never smiled much. Considering Mrs. Hornback, it was not difficult to understand why.

I put the photograph into my coat pocket and got a contract form and filled it in, making sure to add a clause about the five-hundred-dollar bonus. When I gave it to her she read it over three times, the way George Hickox had yesterday, before she affixed her signature. Her scowl as she made out a retainer check was close to being ferocious.

I asked her a few more questions—the address of their

Union Street office, their home address (an apartment on Russian Hill), the make and license number of her husband's car and where he parked it during the day. Then I promised to tender daily reports by phone and got her out of there. The air in the office seemed thinner after she'd gone; she occupied a lot of space, that woman.

With the Speers file in front of me, I planned out an itinerary for the day. Unless I ran into problems, I ought to be able to cover all the legwork possibilities I had established yesterday; and maybe I would get lucky enough to wrap up the Speers thing right away. In any event I figured to be finished in plenty of time to be waiting for Lewis Hornback on Union Street when he quit work at five.

My love life may have been in an uncertain state these days, I thought as I left the office. But business, for once, was booming.

FOUR

At four-fifty that afternoon I was illegally parked in a red-marked bus zone on Union, just off Laguna. Hornback Designs was a block and a half behind me, between Gough and Octavia, and the parking garage where Lewis Hornback kept his Dodge Monaco was just thirty yards ahead. As long as a cop didn't come and chase me away or give me a ticket, I was in a good position to see Hornback coming and to follow him when he left the garage.

I sat with my rearview mirror turned so I could watch the intersection behind me and thought about Kerry. She had been on my mind all day; I kept wondering about that dinner last night with handsome Jim Carpenter, who was Kerry's age and who did not have a beer belly. I had considered stopping somewhere and calling her, but I hadn't got up enough gumption to do it. I would call her at home later on —and not because I wanted to see if she *was* home. Or so I told myself.

The day itself, so far as tracking down the elusive Lauren Speers was concerned, had been a bust. I had talked to her hairdresser, a man named Mr. Ike; I had talked to the head of a local charity she supported; I had talked to a woman she'd gone on a Caribbean cruise with last year and, through her, to Speers's travel agent. Zero. I had also stopped by the Cow Hollow address of her secretary, Bernice Dolan; nobody had been home. Dolan hadn't been there for weeks, according to the building manager, but he didn't know where she'd gone. And her rent was paid through the end of the month, so he didn't seem to care.

I was running out of possibilities, and I wasn't sure what to try next. I could not get my head into figuring angles, at least not now. Later tonight, or tomorrow morning when I checked Brister's file again.

Time passed. People moved up and down the sidewalks, most of them young and on their way to the saloons along the Union strip; this was a popular area, one of the city's current "in" places. The weather had turned almost cold, with scattered clouds, but there was no sign of fog above Twin Peaks or over near the Golden Gate. Which was something of a relief. Tail jobs are tricky enough as it is, especially at night, without the added problem of poor visibility.

Lewis Hornback showed up at 5:04. Which was also a relief; I had been illegally parked long enough not to want to push my luck any further. I recognized him right away. He came walking across Laguna behind me, wearing a light-colored suit, no tie, a gold chain glistening between the open collar wings of his shirt. He looked exactly like his photograph, and he wasn't smiling now, either. He came up onto the sidewalk, drifted past me, and entered the parking garage.

Two minutes later the Dodge Monaco appeared, turned left on Union; I could see Hornback clearly through the windshield when he passed me. He made a right on Laguna and headed up the hill. I gave him a half-block lead before I pulled out into a U-turn and swung up after him.

Where he went was straight out Broadway to North Beach, to a little Italian restaurant not far from Washington Square. I parked a block from where he did, illegally again in another bus zone because there were no other street vacancies, and followed him inside the restaurant. Meeting the girl friend for dinner, maybe, I thought—but that wasn't the way it turned out. After two drinks at the bar, while I nursed a beer, he took a table alone. I sat at an angle across the room from him, treated myself to *pollo al' diavolo,* and watched him pack away a three-course meal and a half-liter of house wine. Nobody came to talk to him except the waiter; he was just a man having a quiet dinner by himself.

He polished off a brandy and three cigarettes for dessert, lingering the way you do after a heavy meal; when he finally left the restaurant it was almost eight o'clock and twilight was settling down on the city. From there he walked over to Upper Grant, where he gawked at the young counterculture types who frequent the area, did a little window-shopping, stopped in at a newsstand and a drugstore. I stayed on the opposite side of the street, fifty yards or so behind him —about as close to a subject as you want to get on foot. But the walking tail got me nothing except exercise: Hornback was still alone when he led me back to where he had left his Dodge.

When I got to my own car there was a parking ticket fluttering under one of the windshield wipers. Terrific. But it was going to wind up being Mrs. Hornback's problem, not mine. As far as I was concerned, things like parking tickets were legitimate expense account items.

Hornback's next stop was a small branch library at the foot of Russian Hill, where he dropped off a couple of books. Then he headed south on Van Ness, west on Market out of the downtown area, and up the winding expanse of Upper Market to Twin Peaks. There was a little shopping area up there, a short distance beyond where Market becomes Portola Drive; he pulled into the lot in front. And went into a neighborhood tavern called Dewey's Place.

I parked down near the end of the lot. Maybe he was meeting the girl friend here or maybe he had just gone into the tavern for a drink; he seemed to like his liquor pretty well. I put on the gray cloth cap I keep in the glove compartment, shrugged out of my coat and turned it inside out—it was one of those reversible models—and put it on again that way. Just in case Hornback had happened, casually, to notice me at the restaurant earlier. Then I stepped out into a cold wind blowing up from the ocean, crossed to Dewey's Place.

Inside, there were maybe a dozen customers, most of them at the bar. Hornback was down at the far end with a drink in one hand and a cigarette in the other—but the stools on both sides of him were empty. And none of the three women in there looked to be unescorted.

So maybe I'd been right and there wasn't a girl friend. It was almost ten o'clock; if a married man has a lady on the side, you'd expect him to get together with her by this time of night. But so far, Hornback had done nothing unusual or incriminating. Hell, he hadn't even done anything interesting.

I sat at the near end of the bar and sipped at a draft beer, watching Hornback in the mirror. He finished his drink, lit a fresh cigarette, and gestured to the bartender for a refill. I thought he looked a little tense, but in the dim lighting I couldn't be sure. He was not waiting for anybody, though, you could tell that: no glances at his watch or at the door. Just killing time, aimlessly? It could be; for all I knew, this was how he spent each of his evenings away from the Russian Hill apartment—eating alone, driving alone, drinking alone. And his reason might be the simplest and most innocent of all: he left the office at five and stayed out until midnight because he didn't want to go home to Mrs. Hornback.

When he'd downed his second drink he stood and reached for his wallet. I had already laid a dollar bill on the bar; I slid off my stool and left ahead of him, so that I was already in my car when he came out.

Now where? I thought as he fired up the Dodge. Another bar somewhere? A late movie? Home early?

None of those. He surprised me by swinging back to the east on Portola and then getting into the left-turn lane for Twin Peaks Boulevard. The area up there was residential, at least on the lower part of the hillside; the road itself wound upward at steep angles, made a figure-eight loop through the empty wooded expanse of Twin Peaks Park, and curled down on the opposite side of the hill.

Hornback stayed on Twin Peaks Boulevard, climbing toward the park. Which meant that he was probably not going to make a house call in the area; he had bypassed the only intersecting streets on this side, and there were easier ways to get to the residential sections below the park to the north.

I wondered if he was just marking more time, if it was his custom to take a long, solitary drive for himself round and about the city before finally heading home.

Since there was almost no traffic I dropped back several hundred feet to keep my headlights out of his rearview mirror on the turns. The view from up there was spectacular; on a night like this you could see for miles on a 360-degree curve—the ocean, the full sweep of the bay, both bridges, the intricate pattern of lights that was San Francisco and its surrounding communities. Inside the park, we passed a couple of cars pulled off on lookouts that dotted the area: people, maybe lovers, taking in the sights.

Hornback went through half the figure eight from east to west, driving without hurry. Once I saw the brief faint flare of a match as he lit another cigarette. When he came out on the far edge of the park he surprised me again: instead of continuing down the hill he slowed and turned to the right, onto a short, hooked spur road where there was another of the lookouts.

I tapped my brakes as I neared the turn, trying to decide what to do. The spur was a dead end; I could follow him around it or I could pull off the road and wait for him to come out again. The latter seemed to be the better choice, and I cut my headlights and started to glide off onto a turnaround. But then, over on the spur, Hornback swung past a row of cypress that lined the near edge of the lookout. The Dodge's brake lights flashed through the screen of trees; then his headlights also winked out.

I kept on going, made the turn and drifted onto a second, tree-shadowed turnaround just beyond the intersection. Diagonally in front of me I could see Hornback ease the Dodge across the flat surface of the lookout, bring it to a stop nose-up against a perimeter guardrail. The distance between us was maybe seventy-five yards.

What's he up to now? I thought. Well, he had probably stopped over there to take in the view and maybe do a little brooding. The other possibility was that he was waiting for someone. A late-evening rendezvous with the alleged girl friend? But the police patrol Twin Peaks Park at regular intervals, because adventuresome kids had been known to use it as a lovers' lane and because there had been trouble in the past with youth gangs attacking parkers. It was hardly the kind of place two adults would pick for an assignation. Why meet up here when the city was full of hotels and motels?

The Dodge gleamed a dullish black in the starlight; there was no moon. From where I was I could see all of the passenger side and the rear third of the driver's side. The interior was shrouded in darkness. Pretty soon another match flamed, smearing the gloom for an instant with dim yellow light. Hornback was not quite a chain-smoker, but he was the next thing to it—at least a three-pack-a-day man. I felt a little sorry for him, considering my own bout with the specter of lung cancer.

I slouched down behind the wheel, tried to make myself comfortable. Five minutes passed. Ten minutes. Fifteen. Behind me, half a dozen sets of headlights came up or went down the hill on Twin Peaks Boulevard; none of them turned in where we were. And nothing moved that I could see in or around the Dodge.

I occupied my mind by speculating again about Hornback. He was a puzzle, all right. Maybe a cheating husband, maybe a thief; maybe an innocent husband and an innocent man—the victim of a loveless marriage and a shrewish wife. He had not done anything of a guilty or furtive nature tonight, and yet here he was, parked alone at 11:10 P.M. on a lookout in Twin Peaks Park. It could go either way. So which way was it going to go?

Twenty minutes.

And I began to feel just a little uneasy. You get intimations like that when you've been a cop as long as I have, vague flickers of wrongness. The feeling made me fidgety; I sat up and rolled down my window and peered across at the Dodge. Stillness. Darkness. Nothing out of the ordinary.

Twenty-five minutes.

The wind was chill against my face, and I rolled the window back up. But the coldness had got into the car; I drew my coat tight around my neck. And kept staring at the Dodge and the bright mosaic of lights beyond, like luminous spangles on the black-velvet sky.

Thirty minutes.

The uneasiness grew, became acute. Something wrong over there. A half-hour was a long time for a man to sit alone on a lookout, whether he was brooding or not; it was even a long time to wait for a rendezvous. But that was only part of the sense of wrongness. Something else . . .

Hornback had not lighted another cigarette since that one nearly a half-hour ago.

The realization made me sit up again. He had been smoking steadily all night long, even during his walk along Upper Grant after dinner. When I was a heavy smoker I could not have gone thirty minutes without lighting up; it seemed funny that Hornback could or would, considering where he was and that there was nothing else for him to do in there. He might have run out, of course—but I remembered seeing a full pack in front of him at Dewey's Place.

What *could* be wrong over there? He was alone in the car, alone up here except for my watching eyes. Nothing could have happened to him. Unless—

Suicide?

The word popped into my mind and made me feel even colder. Suppose Hornback wasn't playing around and suppose he was also despondent over the state of his marriage, maybe over his alleged theft. Suppose all the aimless wandering tonight had been a prelude to an attempt on his own life—a man trying to work up enough courage to kill himself on a lonely road high above the city. It was possible; I didn't know enough about Hornback to be able to judge his mental stability.

I wrapped both hands around the wheel, debating with myself. If I went over and checked on him, and he was all right, I would have blown not only the tail but the job itself. But if I stayed here, and Hornback had taken pills or done Christ knew what to himself, I might be sitting passively by while a man died.

Headlights appeared on Twin Peaks Boulevard behind me. Swung in a slow arc onto the spur road. I drifted lower on the seat and waited for them to pass by.

Only they didn't pass by; the car drew abreast of mine and came to a halt. Police patrol—I sensed that even before I saw the darkened dome flasher on the roof. The passenger window was down, and the cop on that side extended a flashlight through the opening and flicked it on. The light pinned me for three or four seconds, bright enough to make me squint; then it shut off. The patrolman motioned for me to roll down my window.

I glanced past the cruiser at Hornback's Dodge. It remained dark, and there was still no movement anywhere in the vicinity. Well, the decision on whether or not to check on him was out of my hands now; the cops would want to have a look at the Dodge in any case. And in any case the job was blown.

I let out a breath, wound down the glass. The patrolman—a young guy wearing a Prussian mustache—said, "What's going on here, fella?"

So I told him, keeping it brief, and let him have a look at

the photostat of my investigator's license. He seemed half-skeptical, half-uncertain; he had me get out and stand to one side while he talked things over with his partner, a heavyset older man with a beer belly larger than mine. After which the partner took out a second flashlight and trotted across the lookout to the Dodge.

The younger cop asked me some questions and I answered them. But my attention was on the older guy. I watched him reach the driver's door and shine his light through the window. A moment later he appeared to reach down for the door handle, but it must have been locked because I didn't see the door open or him lean inside. Instead he put his light up to the window again. Slid it over to the window on the rear door. And then turned abruptly to make an urgent semaphoring gesture.

"Sam!" he shouted. "Get over here, on the double!"

The young patrolman, Sam, had his right hand on the butt of his service revolver as we ran ahead to the Dodge. I was expecting the worst by this time, only I was not at all prepared for what I saw inside that car. I just stood there gawking while the cops' lights crawled through the interior.

There were spots of drying blood across the front seat.

But the seat was empty, and so was the backseat and so were the floorboards.

Lewis Hornback had disappeared.

FIVE

One of the two inspectors who arrived on the scene a half-hour later was Ben Klein, an old-timer and a casual acquaintance from my own years on the force. I had asked the patrolmen to call in Lieutenant Eberhardt, who was probably my closest friend on or off the cops, because I wanted an ally in case matters became dicey; Eb, though, was evidently still on day shift. I had not asked for Klein, but I felt a little better when he showed up.

When he finished checking over the Dodge we went off to one side of it, near the guardrail. From there I could look down a steep slope dotted with stunted trees and underbrush. Search teams were moving along it with flashlights, looking for some sign of Hornback; so far they didn't seem to be having any luck. Up here, the area was swarming with men and vehicles, most but not all of them official. The usual rubberneckers and media types were in evidence along the spur and back on Twin Peaks Boulevard.

"Let me get this straight," Klein said, frowning, when I was through with my story. He had his hands jammed into his coat pockets and his body hunched against the wind; the night had turned bitter cold now. "You followed Hornback here around ten-forty, and you were in a position to watch his car from the time he parked it to the time the two patrolmen showed up."

"That's right."

"You were on that turnaround?"

"Yes. The whole time."

"And you didn't see anything unusual."

"Nothing at all."

"Could you see inside the car?"

"No—too many shadows."

"But you could see most of the area around it."

"Yes."

"You take your eyes off it for any length of time?"

"A few seconds now and then, no more."

"Were all four doors visible?"

"Three of the four. Not the driver's door."

"That's how he disappeared, then."

I nodded. "But what about the dome light? Why didn't I see it go on?"

"It's not working," Klein said. "Bulb's defective. That was one of the first things I checked after we wired up the door lock."

"I also didn't see the door open," I said. "I might have missed that, I'll admit—but it's the kind of movement that should have attracted my attention." I paused, working my memory. "Hornback couldn't have gone away toward the road or down the embankment to the east or back into those trees over there; I would have seen him if he had. The only other direction is down this slope, right in front of his car. But if that's it, why didn't I notice movement when he climbed over the guardrail?"

"Maybe he didn't climb over it."

"Crawled under it?"

"Maybe."

"Why would he have done that?"

"You tell me."

"Well, I can think of one possibility."

"Which is?"

"The suicide angle," I said. "I told you I was worried about that. What if Hornback decided to do the Dutch, and while he was sitting in the car he used a pocketknife or something else sharp to slash his wrists? That would explain the blood on the front seat. Only he lost his nerve at the last second, panicked, opened the door and fell out of the car and crawled under the guardrail—"

I stopped. The idea was no good; I had realized that even as I laid it out.

Klein knew it, too. He was shaking his head. "No blood outside the driver's door or along the side of the car or anywhere under the guardrail; a man with slashed wrists bleeds pretty heavily. Besides, if he'd cut his wrists and had second thoughts, why leave the car at all? Why not just start it up and drive to the nearest hospital?"

"Yeah," I said.

"There's another funny angle—the locked doors. Who locked them? Hornback? His attacker, if there was an attacker? Why lock them at all?"

I had no answers for him. I stood brooding out at the city lights.

"Assume he was attacked," Klein said. "By a mugger, say, who's decided to work up here because of the isolation. The attacker would have had to get to the car with you watching, which means coming up this slope, along the side of the car, and in through the driver's door."

"And the door would have had to be unlocked when he did it," I said.

"Yeah. Do you buy any of that?"

"No."

"Neither do I. It's TV commando stuff—too farfetched."

"There's another explanation," I said musingly.

"What's that?"

"The attacker was in the car all along."

"Not a mugger, you mean?"

"Right. Somebody who had it in for Hornback."

Klein scowled; he had heavy jowls, and the scowl made him look like a bulldog. "I thought you said Hornback was alone the whole night. Didn't meet anybody."

"He didn't. But suppose he was in the habit of frequenting Dewey's Place, and this somebody knew it. Suppose he —or she— was waiting in the parking lot, slipped inside the Dodge while Hornback and I were in the tavern, hid on the floor in back, and stayed hidden until Hornback came up here and parked. Then maybe stuck a knife in him."

"Also melodramatic, seems to me."

"Me too. But it is possible."

"What kind of motive fits that explanation?"

"How about the money Hornback's wife claims he stole from their firm?"

"You're not thinking the wife attacked him?"

"No. If she was going to do him in, it doesn't make sense she'd hire me to tail him around."

"The alleged girl friend?"

"Could be."

"You said yourself the girl friend might be a figment of the wife's imagination."

I nodded. "But assume she does exist. She could have had a falling-out with Hornback and decided to keep all the money for herself. That kind of thing happens all the time."

"Sure, it does," Klein said, but he sounded dubious. "The main trouble with that idea is, what happened to Hornback's body? The attacker, male or female, would've had to get both himself and Hornback out of the car, then drag the body down the slope. Now, why in hell would somebody kill a man way up here, with nobody around as far as he knew, and take the corpse away with him instead of just leaving it in the car?"

I spread my hands, palms up. "I just can't figure it any other way," I said.

"Neither can I—for now. Let's see what the search teams and the forensic boys turn up."

What the searchers and the lab crew turned up, however, was nothing: no sign of Hornback dead or alive, no sign of anybody else in the area, no bloodstains except for those inside the car, no other evidence of any kind. Hornback— or his body, and maybe an attacker as well—had not only vanished from the Dodge while I was watching it; he had vanished completely and without a trace. As if into thin air.

It was close to 2:00 A.M. before Klein let me go home. He asked me to stop in later at the Hall of Justice to sign a statement, but aside from that he seemed satisfied that I had given him all the facts as I knew them. But I was not quite off the hook yet, nor would I be until Hornback turned up. If he turned up. My word was all the police had for what had happened on the lookout, and I was the first to admit that it was a pretty bizarre story.

When I came into my flat I thought about calling Mrs. Hornback. But on consideration, I saw no point or advantage in phoning a report at this time of night; the police would already have told her about her husband's disappearance. Besides which, I just did not want to talk to the woman or listen to her read me the riot act.

It was too late to call Kerry, too. And even if it wasn't, I was not up to relating the night's events another time to anybody, not without some sleep first.

I drank a glass of milk and crawled into bed and tried to sort things into some kind of order. How had Hornback vanished? Why? Was he dead or alive? An innocent man or as guilty as his wife claimed? The victim of suicidal depression, or of circumstance, or of premeditated violence . . . ?

No good. I was too tired to come up with fresh speculations on any of those questions.

After a while I slept and dreamed a lot of crap about people dematerializing inside locked cars, vanishing in little puffs of smoke. A long time later the telephone woke me up. I keep the thing in the bedroom, and it went off six inches from my ear and sat me up in bed, grumbling. Outside the window, the sky was beginning to lighten, as if blue dye were slowly being added to gray cloth; the nightstand clock said that the time was 6:55. Four hours' sleep and a new day dawning.

The caller, not surprisingly, was Mrs. Hornback. She launched into an immediate harangue, berating me for not getting in touch with her last night; then she demanded my version of what had happened in Twin Peaks Park. I gave it to her.

"I don't believe a word of it," she said.

"That's your privilege, ma'am," I said. "But it happens to be the truth."

"We'll see about that." She sounded even more angry and vituperative than she had in my office yesterday; her voice dripped venom. There was no compassion in the woman, not a whisper of it. "How could you let something like that happen? What kind of detective are you?"

A poor tired one, I thought. "I did what you asked me to, Mrs. Hornback."

"Did you?"

"Yes. What took place on the lookout was beyond my control."

"You just sat there and did nothing," she said. "That's what the police told me."

"If I'd known something was going on—"

"I don't want excuses. I want to know what happened to Lewis; I want the money he stole from me."

"I can't help you on either score," I said. "If I could, I would."

"That bitch of his is mixed up in this," she said. "He was up on Twin Peaks to meet her; he must have been."

"I can't confirm that, Mrs. Hornback. He didn't meet any woman while I was following him—"

"That's what *you* say. You're so observant, you let something happen to him right under your nose." She took a deep breath and let me have her best shot. "This is all your fault, you bum."

"Look, Mrs. Hornback—"

"If my husband isn't found, and if I don't recover my money, you'll hear from my attorney. You can count on that." There was a clattering sound, and the line began to buzz.

Nice lady. A real princess.

I lay back down. I was still half groggy, and pretty soon I went back to sleep. And then the damned phone went off again, sat me up the way it had before. I focused on the clock: 7:40. Conspiracy against my sleep, I thought, not altogether coherently, and fumbled up the handset.

"Wake you up, hotshot?" a familiar voice said with some relish. Eberhardt.

"What do you think?"

"Sorry about that. I've got news for you."

"What news?"

"About that funny business up on Twin Peaks last night."

44

"What about it?"

"Your boy Hornback's been found."

I stopped feeling sleepy; the fuzziness cleared out of my head. "Where?" I said. "Is he all right?"

"In Golden Gate Park," Eberhardt said. "And no, he's not all right. He's dead, been dead since last night sometime. Stabbed in the chest with what was probably a butcher knife."

SIX

I got down to the Hall of Justice at nine-fifteen—showered, shaved, and full of coffee. It was another nice day, clear skies, a little windy. The sunshine softened the austere gray lines of the Hall, made it look less grim than usual. But none of the people on the front steps or in the lobby seemed to be smiling. And neither was I as I rode the elevator up to General Works.

Eberhardt was in his office, gnawing on one of his briar pipes and looking his usual sour self. He was a big, somewhat awkward man, my age, with the general appearance of having been put together with a lot of spare parts, half of them angles and half of them blunt planes. His close-cropped hair was turning gray, and a lot more silver had come into it in the past month. His wife, Dana, had left him for another man, after twenty-eight years of marriage, not long before I'd met Kerry. He had taken it hard and he was

45

still taking it hard; he was not the kind of man who got over things easily.

He avoided my eyes when I came in, as he'd done on each of the half-dozen occasions I had seen him the past few weeks. A week after Dana moved out of their Noe Valley house, he had shown up drunk and disheveled at my flat at 6:00 A.M., after having picked up a woman in a bar and taken her home for the night, and he'd confided that he hadn't been able to perform sexually. It was no major crisis, from a psychological point of view, but for a man like Eberhardt, that kind of failure and that kind of admission had been profound. He wouldn't have told me sober, and I knew he kept brooding about it, and so he had let a certain reserve build up between us. I could not seem to break through it, to get our friendship back to what it had always been.

Looking at him now, I saw that his eyes were bloodshot and his hands just a little unsteady. I wondered if he was still drinking. The last time I'd seen him, two weeks ago, he had told me he was off the booze and coping. But I had my doubts.

He waved me to a chair. "You want some coffee?"

"No. I had some before I left home."

"Suit yourself," he said. "I've been rereading Klein's report. You do get mixed up in the damndest cases."

"Don't I know it."

"One of these days you're going to get in over your head. And you'll wake up some morning with your tail in a sling."

"I play by the rules, Eb, you know that."

"Just the same, you better watch yourself."

"All right."

"Yeah," he said.

I let a small silence build. Then I said, "What have you got on Hornback?"

"Nothing much. Guy out jogging found the body at six-

46

forty, in a clump of bushes along JFK Drive. Stabbed in the chest, like I told you on the phone; single wound that penetrated the heart, probable weapon a butcher knife. ME says death was instantaneous. That takes care of your suicide theory."

"I guess it does."

"No other marks on the body," he said. "Except for a few small scratches on the hands and on one cheek."

"What kind of scratches?"

"Just scratches. The kind you get crawling around in the woods or underbrush—or the kind a body gets if it's been dragged through the same type of terrain. The ME will know more on that when he finishes his postmortem."

"What was the condition of Hornback's clothes?"

"Dirty, torn in a couple of places. Same thing applies."

"Anything among his effects?"

"No. The usual stuff—wallet, handkerchief, change, a pack of cigarettes, and a box of matches. Eighty-three dollars in the wallet and a bunch of credit cards. That seems to rule out a robbery motive."

I said, "I don't suppose there was any evidence where he was found."

"None. Killed somewhere else and then dumped in the park."

"Like up on that Twin Peaks lookout," I said.

"So it would seem. Hornback's blood type was AO; it matches the blood on the front seat of his car."

I watched him break his briar in half and run a pipe cleaner through the stem. The room was too hot; a portable heater rumbled and glowed in one corner. He seemed to crave heat lately, as if he could not get warm—some sort of psychological reaction to his domestic troubles. I could feel sweat forming on my neck and under my arms.

"Hornback's wife thinks you're a bum," he said.

"Yeah, I know. She called me this morning."

"Klein got back a little while ago from breaking the news to her. He says she blames you for her husband's death. He also says she made some thinly veiled accusations."

"What kind of accusations?"

"That maybe you killed Hornback."

"What?"

"On account of you wanted the money he allegedly stole for yourself. She thinks maybe you've got it right now."

"She's crazy," I said. "Christ!"

"Maybe so. But that kind of woman can stir up a lot of trouble. That's what I meant about you waking up some morning with your tail in a sling."

"She can't do anything to me."

"No? Your story is pretty screwy, you know."

"I can't help that. It's the truth."

"Sure. But it's still screwy, and there's still no explanation for what happened to Hornback. If I didn't know you, hot-shot, I'd be taking a pretty close look at you myself right now."

"Come on, Eb. Quit putting the needle in me."

"Is that what you think I'm doing?"

"Isn't it?"

"Ah, go on, get out of here. I got work to do. But listen —keep yourself available. Just in case there are any new developments."

"I'm always available," I said.

"Sure you are. Always."

I stood up, went to the door. When I got there I stopped and turned around. Eberhardt was tamping tobacco into his briar from an oilskin pouch, scowling as he did it.

"Eb . . ."

"No, I haven't heard from Dana," he said without looking up.

48

"Did I ask?"

"You were about to."

" . . . Eb, are you okay?"

"Just dandy."

"I mean—"

"I know what you mean. Don't worry about me."

"But I do. That's what friends are for."

"Worry about your own love life. How's Kerry, by the way?"

"Fine."

He hesitated. And then for the first time he raised his eyes to meet mine, and there was something in them that I could not quite read. "She's a good woman, and you're a lucky bastard to have her," he said. "Keep her happy. Don't let go of her."

A hollow sensation seemed to open up in my stomach. I was careful to keep my voice neutral as I said, "I won't."

"Good. Now go on, beat it. I'm tired of looking at your ugly face."

I went on and beat it.

There were no messages on the answering machine in my office and no mail to speak of. I opened the venetian blinds to let in some sunlight—I needed sunlight this morning, and plenty of it—and then sat down and called Bates and Carpenter.

Kerry wasn't in. "She's gone to an early lunch with Mr. Carpenter," her secretary said. "May I take a message?"

I said, "Just tell her I called."

"Shall I have her return the call?"

"No. I'll get back to her this afternoon."

I swiveled around in my chair and stared out the window. Out to lunch with Jim Carpenter. First dinner, now lunch.

Very cozy. It was just business on Kerry's part, of course—I said that to myself half a dozen times. But what about Carpenter? I knew he wasn't married; Kerry had told me that. What if he was a ladies' man? What if his favorite pastime was screwing his female employees? Kerry hadn't mentioned whether he was that way or not . . . and why hadn't she?

Nuts, I thought. She wouldn't go to bed with him under any circumstances. She'd worked for Bates and Carpenter for over a year; if she was inclined to succumb to Carpenter's charms, whatever the hell they happened to be, she'd have done it long before this. Besides which, she was a monogamous woman, and it was me she was keeping company with these days; she had climbed into the sack with *me* just two days ago, for Christ's sake.

Yeah, I thought, but it wasn't very good for either of us. So maybe she's tired of me and ready to look elsewhere. Maybe she agrees with Ivan the Terrible that she's better off with a young man instead of an old bum. Maybe she *already* succumbed to Carpenter's advances, had an affair with him before I knew her, and now she's weakening again.

Things like that, all sorts of speculations, kept rambling through my head. I couldn't get rid of them, and because I couldn't, I felt stupid and childish and morose. And guilty, too. If she was taking up with Carpenter, or even thinking about taking up with him, it was at least partly my fault. I'd been putting too much pressure on her to marry me. I'd spent too much time bad-mouthing her old man. Ivan the Terrible may have been something of a shit, but he was still her father. How could I blame her if she chose him over me?

I brooded some more. Eberhardt and his marital problems got mixed up in it; I kept drawing parallels between his situation and mine, and I kept hearing him say, "She's a good woman, and you're a lucky bastard to have her. Keep her happy. Don't let go of her." That made me feel even more morose, finally drove me out of the office and down to the restroom at the end of the hall. I looked at myself in the mirror over the sink. Why don't you soak your head, you silly ass, you? I thought. Which seemed like a good idea, so I ran cold water from the tap and went ahead and did it.

When I came back I opened the Speers file again and tried to work. I needed to work; I needed to rechannel my hyperactive imagination. But the first thing that stared up at me was the full-color photograph of Lauren Speers. Red hair like Kerry's, only more flamelike. I turned the photo facedown and picked up one of the newspaper clippings and read the first paragraph six times without any of the words making sense.

The telephone rang.

I hauled up the receiver and said, "Detective agency."

"This is George Hickox. Clyde Mollenhauer's secretary."

Now what? "Yes, Mr. Hickox?"

"About Saturday—Mr. Mollenhauer has an additional request."

"Yes?"

"You're to wear a tuxedo," he said.

"A what?"

"A tuxedo. You do know what a tuxedo is, don't you?"

"I have some idea, yes," I said between my teeth. "May I ask why?"

"Each male guest will be wearing a tux," Hickox said. "Mr. Mollenhauer feels you'd look out of place without one, in the event you should come in contact with any of the guests."

"I see."

"If you don't own a tuxedo, I suggest you make arrangements to obtain one. The requirement is firm."

"I'll rent one right away."

"Do that," he said and hung up in my ear.

I held the receiver at arm's length and gave it the finger. Do *this,* I thought. Which was not very bright; I slammed the thing down. Tuxedo. Me in soup-and-fish and packing a rod, on guard over expensive presents at a wedding reception in Ross. The eighth wonder of the world.

It took me five minutes to find the Yellow Pages; they were hidden away in the back of one file cabinet. I looked up a place that rented tuxedos and gave them a call. The weekend rental fee was fifty dollars, plus a deposit, but that was all right because I was not going to pay for it; Clyde Mollenhauer was going to pay for it. If there was one item that came under the heading of expenses, it was a goddamn tuxedo.

I told the guy what size I wore, arranged to pick up the tux on Friday afternoon, and then went back to the Speers file. The call from Hickox had shaken me out of my mental doldrums, at least; this time I managed to concentrate on what I was reading. Or rereading. No new angles presented themselves—not where Lauren Speers was concerned, anyhow. But I did begin to realize that maybe I had been approaching the hunt from the wrong direction.

None of Speers's relatives or friends might be willing or able to tell me where she'd disappeared to, but what about relatives or friends of Bernice Dolan? Assume Dolan had gone wherever Speers had gone. It was a reasonable assumption; she was Speers's secretary, and the manager of her apartment building had told me she hadn't been home for weeks. All right, then. Find Dolan, and the chances were I would also find Speers.

There was almost no information on Bernice Dolan in the file. I weighed possibilities. The best one seemed to be a canvass of her apartment building; even if none of her neighbors knew where she'd gone, they might be able to provide some useful facts on her background. If that didn't pan out, I could try pumping the *Examiner* society editor again—maybe some of Speers's acquaintances as well. And if that didn't work, I could resort to calling all the Dolans in San Francisco and the other Bay Area counties, on the chance that she was a native and had relatives living here.

I had begun to work up a little enthusiasm by this time. I closed up for the time being, went to where I'd left my car. Getting out was a good idea. It was too damned quiet inside my office. And with Kerry on the one hand, and Edna Hornback and her insinuations on the other, it was too damned noisy inside the dusty cave of my head.

SEVEN

I got lucky for a change. Twenty-five minutes after I arrived at Bernice Dolan's building, I found out where she'd gone.

The building was on Greenwich, over near Fillmore, in the heart of Cow Hollow—a three-story, six-unit job that faced toward the bay. The manager let me in, but he had no additional information for me; he didn't know any of Dolan's friends or any of her background. As far as he was concerned, she kept pretty much to herself.

Her apartment was on the second floor, and there was nobody home in the other apartment across the hall. I went upstairs and talked to a chubby woman with her hair in curlers, who didn't know Dolan at all, or claimed not to, and who thought I was either trying to sell her something or bent on raping her; she kept edging the door closed as we talked, until her nose and mouth were all that were visible beyond an inch-wide crack. Then her face vanished altogether and I heard a couple of locks snap into place. She was definitely not a trusting person.

The second apartment on that floor belonged to a heavy-set bearded guy with long bristly hair and a mashed-in snout, all of which features combined to make him look like a hairy pig. When he opened the door and breathed on me I smelled the odor of sour red wine. Sure, he said, he knew Bernice Dolan. She was a terrific lay, Bernice was; they'd got it on together on Christmas Eve, after a party. Small tits, though, he said. Very small. No, he hadn't seen her recently. Maybe she'd found herself a sugar daddy somewhere, he said, and winked at me. Wouldn't surprise him if she had. She really was a terrific lay, despite her small tits. It was too bad about those tits, he said. Otherwise she would really be a fox.

I left him to his wine and his anatomical hangups and went downstairs again. It was my intention to go all the way down to the first floor, to talk to the occupants of the sixth apartment, but when I got to the second floor I saw a woman with a bag of groceries unlocking the door across from Dolan's. I got over to her just as she popped the door open.

"Excuse me," I said. "I'd like to talk to you for a moment, if I may."

She hadn't seen or heard me coming, and at the sound of my voice she jumped half a foot and almost dropped the bag of groceries. She was about forty, and she had nice brown eyes. That was about all you could say for her in the way of looks; she was so plain and frumpy that I found myself feeling sorry for her. But it was probably just as well, under

the circumstances. At least she didn't think I was there to
rape her.

"My God," she said, "you scared the life out of me."

"I'm sorry. I didn't mean to."

"Well. You shouldn't sneak up on people like that." She
gave me an appraising look. "What did you want?"

"I'm trying to locate Bernice Dolan," I said. "I thought
you might know what's become of her."

"Why do you want to locate Bernice?"

"A small business matter."

"She's not in trouble, is she?"

"Not that I know of. Why do you think she might be?"

"Oh, well, she's a little wild, you know."

"How do you mean?"

"Men," she said. "Bernice is crazy about men." She
paused. "You're not one of them, are you?"

"No, ma'am."

"Good. Don't misunderstand: I like Bernice. It's just that
she's irresponsible. Men and money and fancy possessions,
that's all she ever talks about."

"Do you know her well?"

"Not really. We've talked a few times. I think—" She
stopped, and then shrugged and smiled a faint sad smile. "I
think she likes to talk to me because I'm not a threat to her.
With her men friends, you see. Attractive women often feel
that way about plain women."

I didn't know what to say, so I didn't say anything.

She shrugged again. "Bernice went to Xanadu," she said.

"Ma'am?"

"That's what she said, anyway, the last time I saw her.
That was about three weeks ago. I came home from shopping and she was just coming down the front steps with two
suitcases. I asked her if she was going on vacation and she

55

said not exactly. Then she said she was going to Xanadu."

"Is that all she said?"

"Yes. There was a taxi waiting for her."

"Do you know what Xanadu is? Or where?"

"No. The only Xanadu I know is that newspaper tycoon's estate in *Citizen Kane*. You know—the Orson Welles movie."

I nodded.

"Maybe it's a town or something," the woman said. "Whatever it is, there's one thing it's bound to have plenty of."

"What's that?"

"Men," she said. "Plenty of eligible men."

I thanked her and headed out to my car. Xanadu, I thought. What the hell is Xanadu?

There was a service station two blocks up; I pulled in there and went into their phone booth and looked up Xanadu, just to see what I would find. I didn't find much. The only listing was for some sort of art gallery on Union Street. I thought about driving over there, since Union was only a short distance away, but there didn't seem to be much point in it. A woman doesn't pack two suitcases and call a taxi to go to an art gallery a few blocks from where she lives.

I found a dime in my pocket, dropped it into the coin slot, and rang up the guy I know on the *Examiner*. The first thing he said was, "Another favor, I suppose?" in cynical tones.

I said, "What's Xanadu?"

He said, "Huh?"

"Xanadu. X-a-n-a-d-u."

"What about it?"

"I want to know what it is."

"It's a mythical principality. 'In Xanadu did Kubla Khan a stately pleasure dome decree.' You've heard that before, haven't you? It's from *Kubla Khan*, the Coleridge poem."

56

"I suppose so," I said. "But that's not the Xanadu I'm looking for. The one I want is a place of some kind."

"Well, there's the old tyrant's estate in *Citizen Kane.* Welles patterned him after Willie Hearst, you know—"

"That's not it, either. It's a real place somebody I'm trying to find went to about three weeks ago."

"If you say so."

"No bells ringing?"

"Dead silence," he said.

"Will you check into it for me?"

"Look, I'm pretty busy—"

"I'll buy you a steak dinner."

"When?"

"Next week. You name the night."

He sighed. "All right—but we go to Grisson's."

Grisson's was the most expensive steak restaurant in the city. I wondered if I could get away with putting his dinner on my expense account bill to Adam Brister, decided I would damned well try, and said, "Deal. I'll be back in my office inside an hour. Call me there if you come up with anything."

"I'll see what I can do."

On the way back to Drumm Street I stopped at a McDonald's and bought a Big Mac and a bag of fries. Kerry had accused me of being a junk-food addict, and she was probably right. But what the hell. You have to eat, and you might as well eat what you like. The way I figured it, nobody had ever died from eating a Big Mac and a bag of fries for lunch.

My answering machine had one message on it, from Edna Hornback. She'd called, she wanted me to call back—very terse, very nasty. More abuse, I thought. And up yours, Mrs. Hornback. I erased her voice from the machine, erased her name from my thoughts, and started typing up a report for Adam Brister on the Speers investigation thus far.

I was in the middle of that when Kerry called.

"I was hoping you'd be in," she said. "I'm worried about you."

"Why?"

"Why do you think? You're all over the afternoon paper; I just saw it a little while ago. How come you didn't call to tell me what happened last night?"

"I got home too late," I said. "And I had to go in early this morning to talk to Eberhardt. You'd already gone to lunch when I did get a chance to call."

"I still wish you'd let me know. It was a shock to pick up the paper and see you mixed up in another murder."

"Yeah, I guess it was."

"Have the police found out anything yet?"

"No. But they'll get to the bottom of it eventually." I paused. And then I said, "So did you just get back from lunch?"

"A few minutes ago, yes."

"Kind of a long one, wasn't it?"

"Not really. We had a lot of things to discuss."

"I'm sure you did."

"Now what does that mean?"

"Nothing. It was just a comment."

Silence. Then, "My God, are you jealous?"

"What would I have to be jealous about?"

"Not a thing. But you are, aren't you."

"No," I said.

"Yes you are. I can hear it in your voice."

"Balls," I said. "Let's have dinner tonight."

"I can't."

"Why can't you?"

"Because I can't."

"Another business meeting?"

"That's right. Or don't you think so?"

"Don't get huffy."

"I'm not getting huffy. God, you can be irritating sometimes. What's the matter with you?"

"I'm going through male menopause," I said. "I keep having hot flashes every time I think about you and your friend Carpenter."

"He's not my friend, he's my boss."

"All right."

"All right. You big jerk."

"Balls," I said again.

"Balls to you, too," she said and clanked the receiver down hard enough to make me wince.

I sat there and thought: She's right, I am a big jerk. She calls, worried, and what do I do? Make jealous noises and dumb remarks and get her upset enough to hang up on me. I felt even more like a horse's ass than I had on Sunday. The thing to do was to call her back and apologize. I made up my mind to do that and reached out for the receiver.

Before I could pick it up, the thing went off again.

Maybe she's calling *me* back, I thought, but she wasn't. It was Mrs. Hornback. "Oh, so you're there," she said. "Didn't you get my message?"

"I got it."

"Then why didn't you call me?"

"I had some other things to attend to."

"I'm a grieving widow," she said, but she didn't sound like one. She sounded like the Wicked Witch of the East. "Don't you have any feelings?"

"I might ask you the same question," I said. "I understand you've been making accusations against me to the police."

"I have not been making accusations."

"Inferences, then. You seem to think I had something to do with your husband's death."

"For all I know, you did."

"That's slander, Mrs. Hornback."

"Not if it's true."

"Look, lady, what is it you want? Or did you just call up to harass me?"

"I want what's rightfully mine," she said. "I want the money Lewis stole from Hornback Designs."

"I don't know anything about that."

"Well, you'd better find out."

"What?"

"You'd better find out who has my money and who killed Lewis. You'd better find that bitch of his."

"That's not up to me. It's up to the police."

"The police are incompetent," she said. "You're the only one who can do it." She paused dramatically. "If you're not guilty yourself, that is."

"Are you threatening me?"

"You're still in my employ," she said. "You took my money and you didn't earn it. Well, I'm warning you, you'd better earn it now."

"I have no obligation to you—"

"Of course you do. You claim to be an honest detective. All right, start detecting. That's what I'm paying you for."

I opened my mouth, closed it again. A funny noise came out of my throat—like a dog growling.

She said, "What did you say?"

"I didn't say anything."

"Are you going to find my money and Lewis's killer or aren't you?"

"I don't work for you any longer, Mrs. Hornback."

"If you don't," she said, "it's because you have something to hide. That's how I see it. That's how my attorney sees it, too."

And for the third time that day, somebody banged a telephone receiver down in my ear.

I got up and took a couple of angry turns around the office. The woman was demented; she ought to be locked away in a place with mattresses on the walls. She had just tried to hire me to prove I wasn't a murderer and a thief—that was what the whole crazy conversation amounted to. Great Christ. I had a certifiable lunatic on my hands. The worst kind, too: vindictive and monomaniacal. There was no telling what she might do next.

I sat down again. What I needed right now was an attorney of my own to advise me, before this whole thing got out of hand. I looked up Charles Kayabalian's number in my address book. Kayabalian was an Armenian I had met three years before, during a messy murder case up in the Mother Lode country—a bad time in my life because I had been waiting to find out whether the lesion on my lung was malignant or benign. The case had involved a stolen Oriental rug, and Kayabalian was a collector of Orientals; he was also a very good attorney. I had had occasion to consult with him on minor matters a time or two since.

He was in and free to listen to my tale of woe. When I finished relating it he said in his Melvin Belli voice, "From a legal standpoint, my friend, I doubt if you have much to worry about. The Hornback woman would have to prove felonious intent on your part, and from what you've told me, there's no evidence to substantiate such a claim."

"Could she sue me anyway?"

"Yes. For criminal negligence."

"She couldn't prove that, either."

"Probably not. Any competent judge would throw a suit like that out of court. Still, it could damage you professionally."

"So what do you advise?"

"Don't talk to her anymore," Kayabalian said. "If she calls you again, tell her politely that you have nothing to say to her on advice of counsel and hang up. Meanwhile, I'll get in touch with her and her attorney."

"What will you say to them?"

"You leave that to my discretion. The main thing I want to find out is how serious she is about a potential suit."

I gave him Mrs. Hornback's number. He said he'd be in touch after he talked to her and her lawyer, and to let him know right away if I learned of any fresh developments in the police investigation. He sounded confident enough, but I didn't feel particularly relieved after we rang off. Lunatics make me nervous, attorney or no attorney in my corner.

It had been better than half an hour since my abrasive conversation with Kerry, but I still felt I ought to apologize to her. The only problem with that was when I called Bates and Carpenter her secretary said she was away from her desk and unavailable to take calls. Which may or may not have been true. Maybe she just didn't want to talk to me. Or maybe she was off in Jim Carpenter's private office, conducting more business.

Damn women. And damn me and my petty jealousies.

I put the handset down. Two seconds later the bloody thing's bell went off again. But this time it was my friend on the *Examiner,* and he had some good news.

"I found Xanadu for you," he said. "At least, it's the only one anybody around here knows about."

"What is it?"

"A resort playground for the rich and decadent. Down on the Big Sur seacoast."

"Ah," I said.

"Yeah," he said. "Eighteen-hole golf course, tennis and racquetball courts, Olympic-sized swimming pool, sauna and steam rooms, two restaurants, three bars, a disco night club, and forty or fifty rustic cottages for the guests to hole up in."

"Sounds exclusive."

"It is. The tariff is a mere fifteen hundred per week per person, not including meals, drinks, or gratuities."

"Nice play if you can get it," I said.

"Ain't that the truth. This sound like the Xanadu you're after?"

"I think so."

"Good. That means you won't try to weasel out of my steak dinner next week."

"Any night. Call me on Monday."

"I think I'll have a porterhouse," he said. "Unless there's another steak on the menu more expensive."

I called Monterey County information and got the listed number for Xanadu. Then I called Xanadu and asked to speak to Ms. Lauren Speers. The woman who answered said she would ring up Ms. Speers's cottage, and while she was doing that I hung up. She had already told me what I needed to know; I had found Bernice Dolan and I had found Lauren Speers.

All that remained now was to contact Adam Brister and to drive down the coast to Xanadu with the papers he had given me to serve. I decided I would make the drive first thing tomorrow. A day away from the city, and away from nut cases like Edna Hornback, could only be a blessing.

Brister sounded pleased when I reached him at his office. He told me to contact him again after I had served Speers and that he would issue a check for the balance of my fee, plus expenses, as soon as I presented him with a report and an itemized list. He also said I was a good detective. At least somebody thought so, even if it was only a greedy-eyed member of the bar.

By then it was almost five o'clock, and I was tired of telephones and business matters. I went home to drink beer, read a pulp magazine, and brood in solitude.

Charles Kayabalian called at eight o'clock. "I just returned from dinner," he said. "I tried you at your office at five, but you'd already left."

"Did you talk to Hornback and her attorney?"

"Both of them, yes."

"And?"

"I believe you're right about the woman's mental state," he said. "My conversation with her was a little strange, to say the least."

"Is she serious about a lawsuit?"

"Very serious. Assuming you don't go along with her wishes and find out who killed her husband and what happened to the money she alleges he stole. In her view, that's the only way for you to exonerate yourself."

"What did her attorney have to say?"

"He's backing her one hundred percent. I don't like the man—his name is Jordan and he's an opportunist. He seems to see the matter as a cause célèbre, a way to make a name for himself."

"So what do we do if they go ahead with the suit?"

"File a countersuit for harassment," Kayabalian said. "I see no other alternative."

"Wonderful."

"If the police find out who murdered Lewis Hornback and what happened to the money," he said, "it would probably get you off the hook. We'll just have to hope that happens." He paused. "You *don't* intend to conduct your own investigation, do you?"

"Christ, no."

"Good. It wouldn't be a wise idea. Unless you managed to solve the mystery, Mrs. Hornback's case against you would be strengthened."

"I'll stand clear, don't worry."

He told me again to keep in touch, after which I went back to my beer and my brooding. This was shaping up to be one of the most complicated weeks of my life. I was beginning to think that I had been better off without a lady friend and without a booming business. Love and money were terrific, but peace of mind was a hell of a lot better for you in the long run.

EIGHT

I passed out of the real world, through the portals into Xanadu, at two-fifteen on Wednesday afternoon.

The resort had been built on craggy terrain, among tall redwoods, at the southern end of Monterey County. It was not all that far from the Hearst Castle at San Simeon, which tied off one of the historical references for its name; my steak-eating pal on the *Examiner* had told me that William Randolph Hearst was the model for the newspaper tycoon in *Citizen Kane*. Xanadu's grounds extended out to sheer cliffs that fell away to the Pacific. I had the window rolled down —it was a warm day down here, if a little windy—and as I followed an access road that wound upward past part of the golf course, I could smell the clean salt tang of the sea and hear the faint crash of surf in the distance.

The ride down from San Francisco had been more or less soothing. I had got up early, after not much sleep, and I had been in a foul humor. A call to the Hall of Justice had not helped it any; Eberhardt hadn't come in yet, but Klein was there and I found out from him that there was nothing new on the Hornback murder. If Lewis Hornback *had* had a girl friend, he said, they hadn't been able to dig up any trace of her.

After that I had called Kerry at her apartment and finally made my apologies for the way I'd acted on the phone yesterday. She had accepted them all right and seemed cheerful enough, but I sensed the distance again. She had agreed to have dinner with me tomorrow night, which was something of a relief; I would be able to get a better handle on the situation face to face with her. Still, that vague sense of distance continued to bother me.

So the foul humor had persisted as I left the city and headed south. It lasted until I came over the Santa Cruz Mountains and picked up Highway One. The drive down One, past Monterey and Cypress Bay and along the rim of the ocean, was one of the most scenic in the state: rugged cliffs and promontories, deep canyons, Monterey cypress trees wind-twisted into myriad shapes, the wooded slopes of the Santa Lucia Range and the Los Padres National Forest, the sunlit Pacific stretching away to the horizon. You would have had to be mired in depression not to respond to all that nature-in-the-raw, and I was not that bad off—not yet, anyway. Now, entering Xanadu, I felt a little more optimistic about things, my relationship with Kerry included.

The access road curled among lush redwoods and giant ferns, emerged into a parking area shaped like a bowl. Three-quarters of it was reserved for guest parking; the other quarter was taken up with rows of three-wheeled machines that looked like golf carts, with awnings over them done in pastel ice-cream colors. From what I had been told about Xanadu, the carts were probably used by guests to get from one of the complex's pleasure domes to another. Exercise was all well and good in its proper place—tennis court, swimming pool, disco—but the rich folk no doubt considered walking up and down hilly terrain a vulgarity.

Beyond where the carts were was a long slope, with a wide path cut into it and a set of stairs alongside that seemed more ornamental than functional. At the top of the slope, partially visible from below, were some of the resort buildings, all painted in pastel colors like the cart awnings. The muted sounds of people at play drifted down on the cool breeze from the ocean.

I put my car into a slot marked *Visitors' Parking.* A black guy in a starched white uniform came over to me as I got out. He was about my age, with a lot of gray in his hair, and his name was Horace. Or so it said on the pocket of his uniform, in pink script like the sugar writing on a birthday cake.

He looked at me and I looked at him. I was wearing my best suit, but my best suit was the kind the inhabitants of Xanadu would wear to costume parties or give away to the Salvation Army. But that was okay by Horace. Some people who work at fancy places like this get to be snobs in their own right; not him. His eyes said that I would never make it up that hill over yonder, not for more than a few minutes at a time, but then neither would he, and the hell with it.

I let him see that I felt the same way, which earned me a faint smile in return. "Here on business?" he asked.

"Yes. I'm looking for Lauren Speers."

"She's out right now. Took her car a little past one."

"Do you have any idea when she'll be back?"

"Depends on how thirsty she gets, I expect."

"Pardon?"

"The lady drinks," Horace said and shrugged.

"So I've heard."

"As much as anybody I ever saw," he said. "She's a world-champion drinker, that lady."

"Had she been drinking before she left?"

He nodded. "Martinis. Starts in at eleven every morning, quits at one, sleeps until four. Then it's Happy Hour. But not today. Today she decided to go out. If I'd seen her in time, I'd have tried to talk her out of driving, but she was in that sports job of hers and gone before I even noticed her."

"Must be nice to be rich," I said.

"Yeah," he said.

"Can you tell me which cottage is hers?"

"Number Forty-one. Straight ahead past the swimming pool. Paths are all marked. Miss Dolan'll likely be there if you want to wait at the cottage."

"That would be Bernice Dolan."

"Yep. Miss Speers's secretary. She's writing a book, you know. Miss Speers, I mean."

"I heard that, too. Do you know what kind of book?"

"All about her life. Ought to be pretty spicy."

"From what I know about her, I guess it will be."

"But I'll never read it," Horace said. "Bible, now, that's much more interesting. If you know what I mean."

I said I knew what he meant. And thanked him for his help. I didn't offer him any money; if I had, he would have been offended. He would take gratuities from the guests because that was part of his job, but it had already been established that he and I were social equals. And that made an exchange of money unseemly.

I climbed the stairs—I wouldn't have driven one of those cute little carts even if it was allowed, which it wasn't or Horace would have offered me one—and found my way to the swimming pool. You couldn't have missed it; it was laid out between the two largest buildings, surrounded by a lot of bright green lawn and flagstone terracing, with a stone-faced outdoor bar at the near end. Twenty or thirty people in various stages of undress occupied the area. A few of them were in the pool, but most were sitting at wrought-iron tables, being served tall drinks by three white-jacketed waiters. None of the waiters, I noticed, was black.

Nobody paid any attention to me as I passed by, except for a hard-looking thirtyish blonde who undressed me with her eyes—women do it, too, sometimes—and then put my clothes back on and threw me out of her mental bedroom. A fiftyish lone wolf with shaggy looks and a beer belly was evidently not her type.

Past the pool area, where the trees began again, were a pair of paths marked with redwood-burl signs. The one on the left, according to the sign, would take me to Number Forty-one, so I wandered off in that direction. Ten minutes later I was still wandering, uphill now, with Forty-one still nowhere in sight. I was beginning to realize that the fancy little carts were not such an affectation as I had first taken them to be.

I had passed three cottages so far—or the walks that led to three cottages. The buildings themselves were set back some distance from the main path, half-hidden by trees, and were all lavish chalet types with wide porches and pastel-colored wrought-iron trim. Unlike the stairs from the parking area, the wrought iron was just as functional as it was ornamental: the curved bars and scrollwork served as a kind of burglar proofing over the windows. Xanadu may have been a whimsical pleasure resort, but its rulers nonetheless had their defenses up.

Here in the woods it was much cooler, almost cold, because of the ocean breeze and because the afternoon sunlight penetrated only in dappled patches. I was wishing that I'd worn a coat over my suit when I came around a bend and glimpsed a fourth cottage through the redwoods. Another burl sign stood adjacent to the access path, and I could just make out the numerals *41* emblazoned on it.

I took a few more steps toward the sign. Then, from behind me, I heard a sound like that of a lawnmower magnified —one of the carts approaching. I moved off the path as the sound grew louder. A couple of seconds later the thing came around the curve at my back, going at an erratic clip, and shot past me. Inside at the wheel was a redhaired woman wearing white.

The cart veered over to Forty-one's walk, slowed to a stop, and the redhead got out and hurried toward the cottage. The white garment she wore was a thin coat, buttoned up against the wind, and she had a big straw bag in her right hand; the long red hair streamed out behind her like a sheet of flame. The way she'd handled the cart indicated Lauren Speers was every bit as sloshed as Horace had led me to believe, but she carried herself on her feet pretty well. The serious drinker, male or female, learns how to walk, if not drive, in a straight line.

I called out to her, but she either didn't hear me or chose to ignore me; she kept on going without breaking stride or even glancing in my direction. I ran the rest of the way to the cottage path, turned in along it. She was already on the porch by then, digging in her bag with her free hand; I could see her through a gap in the fronting screen of trees. She found a key and had it in the lock before I could open my mouth to call to her again. In the next second she was inside, with the door shut behind her.

Well, hell, I thought.

I stopped and spent thirty seconds or so catching my breath. Running uphill had never been one of my favorite activities, even when I was in good physical shape. Then I hauled out the subpoena Adam Brister had given me to serve. And then I started along the path again.

I was twenty yards from the porch, with most of the cottage visible ahead of me, when the gun went off.

It made a flat cracking sound in the stillness, muffled by the cottage walls but distinct enough to be unmistakable. I pulled up, stiffening, the hair bristling like cat's fur on my neck. There was no second shot, not in the three or four seconds I stood motionless and not when I finally went charging up onto the porch.

I swatted the door a couple of times with the edge of my hand. Nothing happened inside. But after a space there was a low cry and a woman's voice said querulously, "Bernice? Oh my God—Bernice!" I caught hold of the knob, turned it; it was locked. This was no time to observe the proprieties. I stepped back a pace and slammed the bottom of my shoe against the latch just below the knob.

Metal screeched and wood splinters flew; the door burst open. And I was in a dark room with redwood walls, a beamed ceiling, a fireplace along one wall, rustic furniture scattered here and there. Off to the left was a dining area and a kitchen; off to the right was a short hallway that would lead to the bedrooms and the bath. I saw all of that peripherally. The main focus of my attention was the two women in the room, one of them lying crumpled on a circular hooked rug near the fireplace, the other one standing near the entrance to the hallway. Equidistant between them, on the polished wood floor at the rug's perimeter, was a small-caliber automatic.

The standing woman was Lauren Speers. She had shed the white coat—it was on the couch with her straw bag—and she was wearing shorts and a halter, both of them white and brief, showing off a good deal of buttery tan skin. She stood without moving, staring down at the woman on the rug, the knuckles of one hand pressing her lips flat against her teeth.

Her expression was one of bleary shock, as if she had too much liquor inside her to grasp the full meaning of what had happened here. Or to have registered my violent entrance. Even when I moved deeper into the room, over in front of her, she did not seem to know I was there.

I went for the gun first. You don't leave a weapon lying around on the floor after somebody has just used it. I picked it up by the tip of the barrel—it was a .25 caliber Beretta and still warm to the touch—and dropped it into my coat pocket. Lauren Speers still didn't move, still didn't acknowledge my presence; her eyes were half rolled up in their sockets. And I realized that she had fainted standing up, that it was only a matter of seconds before her legs gave out and she fell.

Before that could happen I put an arm around her waist and half-carried her to the nearest chair, put her into it. She was out, all right; her head lolled to one side. I could smell the stale odor of gin on her breath. The whole room smelled of gin, in fact, as if somebody had been using the stuff for disinfectant.

The woman on the rug was dead. I knew that even without checking for a pulse; had known it the instant I saw her wide-open eyes and the blood on her blouse beneath one twisted arm. She was in her late twenties, attractive in a regular-featured way, with short black hair and a Cupid's-bow mouth. Wearing blouse, skirt, open-toed sandals.

I stood staring down at her, the way Speers had. My stomach felt queasy; a mixture of revulsion and awe had taken a grip on my mind. It was the same reaction I always had to violent death, because it was such an ugliness, such a waste. But there was more to it than that in this case—a resentment of the vagaries of fate, and a kind of fear.

For the second time this week I had stumbled smack into the middle of a homicide.

NINE

Lauren Speers was still sprawled where I'd put her in the chair, unmoving. I went past her, down the short hall, and looked into the two bedrooms and the bath. All three were empty. And the windows in all three were closed and locked; I could see that at a glance.

I came back out and looked into the kitchen. That was empty, too. I started across to a set of sliding glass doors that led onto a rear balcony, but before I got there I noticed something on the floor between the couch and a burl coffee table—a piece of white paper folded lengthwise, lying there tent-fashion. I detoured over and used my handkerchief to pick it up.

It was a sheet of notepaper with six lines of writing in a neat, backslanted feminine hand: three names followed by three series of numbers. All of the names and numbers had heavy lines drawn through them, like items crossed off on a grocery list.

Rykman 56 57 59 62 63 116–125 171–175—25,000
Boyer 214–231 235 239–247 255—25,000
Huddleston 178 180 205–211 360–401 415–420—50,000

None of that meant anything to me. I put the paper into the same pocket with the gun, moved on to the sliding doors.

They were securely locked, with one of those dead-bolt latches that are supposed to be impossible to force from outside. Adjacent was a wide dormer-style window split into vertical halves that fastened in the center, so you could open them inward on a hot day to let in the sea breeze. The halves were also locked—a simple bar-type catch on one that flipped over and fit inside a bracket on the other—and there was more of the wrought-iron burglar proofing bolted over them on the outside.

I stood at the glass doors, peering out. From there you had an impressive view down a long rocky slope to where the Pacific roiled up foam in a secluded cove, framed on both sides by skyscraping redwoods. But it wasn't the view that had my attention; it was what appeared to be a strip of film, about three inches in length, that was caught on a railing splinter off to one side and fluttering in the wind. I debated whether or not to unlatch the doors and go out there for a closer look. I was still debating when somebody came clumping up onto the front porch.

The noise brought me around. The front door was still open, and I watched it fill up with six feet of a youngish, flaxen-haired guy dressed in tennis whites and carrying a covered racquet. He said, "What's going on here? Who are you?" Then he got to where he could see the body on the rug, and Lauren Speers unconscious in the chair, and he said, "Christ!" in an awed voice.

Right away, to avoid trouble, I told him my name, my profession, and the fact that I had come to Xanadu to see Lauren Speers on a business matter. Then I asked him, "Who would you be?"

"Joe Craig." He seemed stunned, confused; his eyes kept shifting away from me to the body. "I work here—I'm one of the tennis pros."

I gestured at the racquet in his hand. "Is that why you came by just now?"

"Yes. Ms. Speers and I had a three o'clock tennis lesson. My cottage is nearby, and I was going to ride down to the courts with her."

There was a telephone on another burl table beside the couch. I went to it and rang up the resort office. And spent five minutes and a lot of breath explaining three times to three different people that there had been a shooting in Number Forty-one and somebody was dead. None of the three wanted to believe it. A killing in Xanadu? Things like that just didn't happen. The first one referred me to the second, and the second to the third; the third guy, who said he was Resident Director Mitchell, maintained his disbelief for a good two minutes before a kind of horrified indignation took over and he promised to notify the county police immediately.

Craig had gone over to Lauren Speers and was down on one knee beside her, chafing one of her hands. "Maybe we should take her outside," he said. "Let her have some air."

That was a reasonable suggestion. I helped him get her up out of the chair, and as we hauled her across to the door I asked him, "Do you know the dead woman?"

"God, yes. Bernice Dolan, Ms. Speers's secretary. Did Ms. Speers do that to her? Shoot her like that?"

"So it would seem." On the porch we put her onto a wrought-iron chaise longue, and Craig went after her hand again. "There's nobody else here, the balcony doors and all the windows are locked from the inside, and I was down on the path with a clear look at the front door when it happened."

He shook his head. "I knew they weren't getting along,"

he said, "but I never thought it would lead to anything like this."

"How did you know they weren't getting along?"

"Bernice told me."

"Did you know her well?"

"We dated a couple of times—nothing serious." Another headshake. "I can't believe she's dead."

"What was the trouble between them?"

"Well, Ms. Speers is writing a book. Or rather, dictating one. All about some of the important people she's known and some of the things she's been mixed up in, in the past."

"Such as?"

"I don't know. But the book is full of scandalous material, apparently. She'd got her hands on all sorts of letters and documents, and she quoted some of them at length. Bernice'd had some editorial experience in Los Angeles and kept telling her she couldn't do that because some of the material was criminal and most of it was libelous. But that didn't seem to matter to Ms. Speers; she said she was going to publish it anyway, if she had to pay for it herself. They were always arguing about it."

"Why didn't she just fire Bernice?"

"I guess she was afraid Bernice would go to some of the people mentioned in the book, out of spite or something, and stir up trouble."

"Were their arguments ever violent?"

"I think so. Bernice was afraid of her. She'd have quit herself if she hadn't needed the money."

But even if Lauren Speers was prone to violence, I thought, why would she shoot her secretary no more than two minutes after returning from an after-lunch drive? That was how long it had been between the time I saw her go inside and the time the gun went off: two minutes, maximum.

Craig's hand chafing was finally having an effect. Speers made a low moaning sound, her eyelids fluttered and slid up, and she winced. Her stare was glassy and blank for three or four seconds; the pupils looked as if they were afloat in bloody milk. Then memory seemed to come back to her and her eyes focused, her body jerked as if an electrical current had passed through it.

"Oh my God!" she said. "Bernice!"

"Easy," Craig said. "It's all over now."

"Joe? What are you doing here?"

"Our tennis date, remember?"

"I don't remember anything. Oh God, my head . . . " Then she saw me standing there. "Who're you?"

We got it established who I was and more or less why I was present. She did not seem to care; she pushed herself off the chaise longue before I was done talking and went inside. She was none too steady on her feet, but when Craig tried to take her arm she smacked his hand away. One long look at the body produced a shudder and sent her rushing into the kitchen. I heard the banging of cupboard doors, the clink of glassware; a few seconds later she came back with a cut-glass decanter in her right hand and an empty tumbler in her left. The decanter was full of something colorless that was probably gin.

I went over as she started to pour and took both decanter and tumbler away from her. "No more liquor," I said. "You've had plenty."

Her eyes snapped at me, full of sudden savagery. "You fat son of a bitch—how dare you! Give it back to me!"

"No," I said, thinking: Fat son of a bitch. Yeah. I put my back to her and went down the hall into the bathroom. She came after me, calling me more names; clawed at my arm and hand while I emptied the gin into the washbasin. I yelled to Craig to get her off me, and he came and did that.

There was blood on the back of my hand where she'd scratched me. I washed it off, dabbed the scratch with iodine from the medicine cabinet. Speers was back on the chaise longue when I returned to the porch, Craig beside her looking nonplussed. She was shaking and she looked sick, shrunken, as if all her flesh had contracted inside her skin. But the fury was still alive in those green eyes; they kept right on ripping away at me.

I asked her, "What happened here today?"

"Go to hell," she said.

"Why did you kill Bernice Dolan?"

"Go to—What? My God, you don't think *I* did it?"

"That's how it looks."

"But I didn't, I couldn't have . . . "

"You were drunk," I said. "Maybe that explains it."

"Of course I was drunk. But I don't kill people when I'm drunk. I go straight to bed and sleep it off."

"Except today, maybe."

"I told you, you bastard, I didn't kill her!"

"Look, lady, I'm tired of you calling me names. I don't like it and I don't want to listen to it anymore. Maybe you killed your secretary and maybe you didn't. If you didn't, then you'd better start acting like a human being. The way you've been carrying on, you look guilty as sin."

She opened her mouth, shut it again. Some of the heat faded out of her eyes. "I didn't do it," she said, much calmer, much more convincing.

"All right. What did happen?"

"I don't know. I heard the shot, I came out of the bedroom, and there she was all twisted and bloody, with the gun on the floor. . . . "

"A .25 caliber Beretta. Your gun?"

"Yes. My gun."

"Where do you usually keep it?"

"In the nightstand in my bedroom."

"Did you take it out today for any reason?"

"No."

"Did Bernice have it when you got back?"

A blank look. "Got back?"

"From wherever you went this afternoon."

"Away from Xanadu? In my car?"

"Are you saying you don't remember?"

"Okay, I have memory lapses sometimes when I've been drinking. Blackouts—an hour or two. But I don't normally go out driving . . ."

The misery in her voice made her sound vulnerable, almost pathetic. I still didn't like her much, but she was in a bad way—physically, emotionally, and circumstantially—and she needed all the help she could get. Beginning with me. Maybe.

I said, "You normally come back here, is that right?"

"Yes. I thought that's what I did today, after lunch. I remember starting back in the cart . . . but that's all. Nothing else until I heard the shot and found Bernice."

Out on the main path I heard the whirring of an oncoming cart. A short time later two middle-aged guys, both dressed in expensive summer suits, came running through the trees and up onto the porch. The taller of them, it developed, was Resident Director Mitchell; the other one, short and sporting a caterpillarlike mustache, was Xanadu's chief of security.

The first thing they did was to go inside and gape at the body. When they came out again I explained what had happened so far as I knew it, and what I was doing in Xanadu in the first place. Speers did not react to the fact that I'd come to serve her with a subpoena. Death makes every other problem inconsequential.

She had begun to look even sicker; her skin had an unhealthy grayish tinge. When Mitchell and the security chief moved off the porch for a conference, she got up and hurried into the cottage. I went in after her, to make sure she didn't touch anything or go for another stash of gin. But it was the bathroom she wanted this time; five seconds after she shut the door, retching sounds filtered out through it.

I stepped into her bedroom and took a turn around it without putting my hands on any of its surfaces. The bed was rumpled, and the rest of the room looked the same— scattered clothing, jars of cosmetics, bunches of dog-eared paperback books. There were also half a dozen framed photographs of well-groomed men, all of them signed with the word "love."

The retching noises had stopped when I came out, and I could hear water running in the bathroom. I moved down to the other, smaller bedroom. Desk with an electric portable typewriter and a dictating machine on its top. No photographs and nothing much else on the furniture. No sign of a manuscript, either; that would be locked away somewhere, I thought.

The sliding closet door was ajar, so I put my head through the opening. The closet was empty except for two bulky suitcases. I nudged both with my foot and both seemed to be packed full.

Half a minute after I returned to the living room, Lauren Speers reappeared. When she saw me she ducked her head and said, "Don't look at me, I look like hell." But I looked at her anyway. I also blocked her way to the door.

Using my handkerchief, I took out the piece of notepaper I had found earlier and held it up where she could see what was written on it. "Do you have any idea what this is, Ms. Speers?" She started to reach for it, but I said, "No, don't touch it. Just look."

She looked. "I never saw it before," she said.

"Is the handwriting familiar?"

"Yes. It's Bernice's."

"From the looks of it, she was left-handed."

"Yes, she was. If that matters."

"The three names here—are they familiar?"

"Yes. James Huddleston is the former state attorney general. Edward Boyer and Samuel Rykman are both prominent businessmen."

"Close friends of yours?"

Her mouth turned crooked. "Not anymore."

"Why is that?"

"Because they're bastards."

"Oh?"

"And one is an out-and-out thief."

"Which one?"

She shook her head—there was a feral gleam in her eyes now—and started past me. I let her go. Then I put the paper away again, followed her onto the porch.

The security chief had planted himself on the cottage path to wait for the county police; Craig was down there with him. The resident director had disappeared somewhere, probably to go do something about protecting Xanadu's reputation. Nobody was paying any attention to me, so I went down and along a packed-earth path that skirted the far side of the cottage.

At the rear there were steps leading up onto the balcony. I climbed them and took a look at the strip of film I had noticed earlier, caught on a wood splinter through one of several small holes along its edge. It was the stiff and sturdy kind they use to make slides—the kind that wouldn't bend easily under a weight laid on it edgewise.

I paced around for a time, looking at this and that. Then I stood still and stared down at the ocean spray boiling over the rocks below, not really seeing it, looking at some things inside my head instead. I was still doing that when more cart noises sounded out front, two or three carts this time, judging from the magnified whirring and whining. County cops, I thought. Nice timing, too.

When I came back around to the front two uniformed patrolmen, a uniformed officer in captain's braid, a civilian carrying a doctor's satchel, and another civilian with photographic equipment and a field lab kit were being met by the security guy. I walked over and joined them.

The captain, whose name turned out to be Orloff, asked me, "You're the private detective? The man who found the body?"

"That's right." I relinquished the .25 caliber Beretta, saying that I had only handled it by the barrel. Not that it would have mattered if I *had* taken it by the grip; if there were any fingerprints on it, they would belong to Lauren Speers.

"It was just after the shooting that you arrived?" Orloff asked.

"Not exactly. I was in the vicinity before the shooting. I broke inside after I heard the shot—not much more than a minute afterward."

"So you didn't actually see the woman shoot her secretary."

"No. But I wouldn't have seen that if I'd been inside when it happened. Ms. Speers didn't kill Bernice Dolan."

"What? Then who did?"

"The man standing right over there," I said. "Joe Craig."

TEN

There was one of those sudden electric silences. Both Craig and Lauren Speers were near enough to hear what I'd said; he stiffened and gaped at me, and she came up out of her chair on the porch. Craig's face tried to arrange itself into an expression of innocent disbelief, but he was not much of an actor; if this had been a Hollywood screen test, he would have flunked it hands down.

He said, "What the hell kind of crazy accusation is that?" Which was better—more conviction—but in my ears it still sounded false.

His guilt was not so obvious to Orloff or any of the others. They kept looking from Craig to me as if trying to decide whom to believe. But I was on pretty firm ground; I would not have accused Craig publicly unless I thought so. The fear I'd felt earlier was gone. The Hornback murder still had me wrapped up in the middle, but this one, at least, was going to be resolved in a hurry.

The security guy said, "How could Joe be guilty? The balcony door and each of the windows are locked from the inside; you said so yourself. You also said there was no one else in the cottage except Ms. Speers and the dead woman when you broke in."

"That's right," I said. "But Craig wasn't in the cottage

when he shot Bernice Dolan. And everything wasn't locked up tight, either."

Craig said, "Don't listen to him, he doesn't know what he's talking about—"

"The living room smells of gin," I said to the security guy. "You must have noticed that when you were in there. It smelled just the same when I first went in. But if you fire a handgun in a closed room, you get the smell of cordite. No cordite odor means the gun was fired outside the room."

"That's true enough," Orloff said. "Go on."

"I'd been here less than ten minutes when Craig showed up. He claimed he'd come to keep a tennis date with Ms. Speers. But the parking lot attendant told me earlier that she drinks her lunch every day and then comes here to sleep it off until Happy Hour at four o'clock. People on that kind of heavy-drinking schedule don't make dates to go play tennis at three."

That also made sense to Orloff and the others; a couple of them cast sidelong glances at Craig.

"He said something else, too—much more damning. When I asked him if he knew the dead woman, he identified her as Bernice Dolan. Then he said, 'Did Ms. Speers do that to her? Shoot her like that?' But I didn't say anything about hearing a gunshot until later; and the way the body is crumpled on the rug, with one arm flung over the chest, all you can see is blood, not the type of wound. So how did he know she was shot? She could just as easily have been stabbed to death."

There was not much bravado left in Craig; you could almost see him wilting, like an uprooted weed drying in the sun. "I assumed she was shot," he said weakly. "I just . . . assumed it."

Lauren Speers had come down off the porch and was staring at him. "Why?" she said. "For God's sake, *why*?"

He shook his head at her. But I said, "For the money, that's why. A hundred thousand dollars in extortion payoffs, at least some of which figures to be in his own cottage right now."

That pushed Craig to the breaking point. He backpedaled a couple of steps and might have kept right on backing if one of the patrolmen hadn't grabbed his arm.

Lauren Speers said, "I don't understand. What extortion?"

"From those three men I asked you about a few minutes ago—Huddleston, Boyer, and Rykman. They figure prominently in the book you're writing, don't they? Large sections of it are devoted to them, sections that contain material either scandalous or criminal?"

"How do you know about that?"

"Craig told me; he was trying to make it seem like you had a motive for killing Bernice. And you told me when you said those three men were bastards and one of them was an out-and-out thief. This little piece of paper took care of the rest."

I fished it out of my coat pocket again as I spoke, handed it to Orloff. He looked at it and then said, "What do all these numbers mean?"

"The first series after each name are page numbers—pages in the book manuscript, pages on which the most damaging material about that person appears. The numbers after the dash are the amounts extorted from each man."

"Where did you get this?"

"It was on the floor between the couch and the coffee table. Right near where Ms. Speers's bag was. I think that's where it came from—out of the handbag."

She said, "How could it have been in my bag?"

"Bernice put it there. While she was out impersonating you this afternoon."

Now everybody looked bewildered. Except Craig, of

course; he only looked trapped and sick, much sicker than Lauren Speers had earlier.

"Impersonating me?" she said.

"That's right. Wearing a red wig and your white coat, and carrying your bag. You didn't go anywhere after lunch except back here to bed; it was Bernice who took your Porsche and left Xanadu. And it was Bernice who passed me in the cart, Bernice I saw enter the cottage a couple of minutes before she was shot."

The security guy asked, "How can you be sure about that?"

"Because Bernice was left-handed."

"I don't see—"

"Ms. Speers is right-handed," I said. "I could tell that a while ago when she started to pour from a decanter into a glass—decanter in her right hand, glass in her left. But the woman who got out of the cart carried the straw bag in her right hand, and when she got to the cottage door she used her left hand to take out the key and to open the door."

Lauren Speers looked at a lock of her red hair, as if to make sure it was real. "Why would Bernice impersonate me?"

"She and Craig were in on the extortion scheme together, and it was part of the plan. They must have worked it something like this. As your secretary she had access to your book manuscript, your personal stationery, your signature, and no doubt your file of incriminating letters and documents. She also had access to your personal belongings and your car keys, particularly from one to four in the afternoons while you were sleeping. And she'd have known from your records how to contact Huddleston and the other two.

"So she and Craig wrote letters to each of them, on your stationery over your forged signature, demanding large sums of money to delete the material about them from your book and to return whatever documents concerned them; they probably also enclosed photocopies of the manuscript pages and the documents as proof. The idea was to keep themselves completely in the clear if the whole thing backfired. You'd get the blame in that case, not them.

"To maintain the illusion, Bernice had to pretend to be you when she collected the payoffs. I don't know what sort of arrangements she and Craig made, but they wouldn't have allowed any of the three men to deliver the money personally. An intermediary, maybe, someone who didn't know you. Or maybe a prearranged drop site. In any event, Bernice always dressed as you at collection time."

Orloff asked, "Why do you think Craig killed her?"

"The old double cross," I said. "They'd collected all the extortion money; that's evident from the way each of the three names is crossed out on that paper. Today was the last pickup, and I think they had it worked out that she would resign from Speers's employ and Craig would resign from Xanadu and they'd go off somewhere together. Her closet is all cleaned out, and her bags are packed."

"But Craig had other ideas?"

I nodded. "He knew when she was due back here, and he was waiting for her—outside on the rear balcony. When she let herself in he knocked on the window and gestured for her to open the two halves. After she did that he must have said something like, 'Quick, lock the front door, take off the coat, and give me the wig and the money.' She'd have thought there was some reason for the urgency, and she trusted him; so she did what he asked. And when she pulled the money out of the handbag she also pulled out the slip of paper. In her haste it fell to the floor, unnoticed.

"As soon as Craig had the wig and the money he took out

the Beretta, which he'd swiped from Speers's nightstand, and shot Bernice. And then threw the gun inside and pulled the halves of the window closed."

"And locked them somehow from the outside," the security guy said, "in the minute or two before you broke in? How could he do that?"

"It wasn't all that difficult, considering the catch on those window halves is a bar type that flips over into a bracket. The gimmick he used was a thin but stiff strip of film. He lost it afterward without realizing it; you'll find it still caught on a splinter on the balcony railing.

"The way he did it was to insert the filmstrip between the two halves and flip the catch over until it rested on the strip's edge. Then he pulled the halves all the way closed, using his thumb and forefinger on the inner frames of each, and with his other hand he eased the strip downward until the catch dropped into the bracket. And then he withdrew the strip from the crack. With a little practice you could do the whole thing in thirty seconds.

"So far he had himself a perfect crime. He'd only have had to return to his cottage, get rid of the wig, stash the money, pick himself up a witness or two, and come back here and 'find' Speers locked up with the body. Under the circumstances he'd arranged, she would be the only one who could have committed the murder.

"What screwed him up was me showing up when I did. He heard me pounding on the door as he was working his trick with the filmstrip; he had just enough time to slip away into the woods before I broke in. But who was I? What had I seen and heard? The only way he could find out was to come back as soon as he'd dumped the wig and money. The fact that he showed up again in less than ten minutes means he didn't dump them far away; they won't be hard to find.

There might even be a fingerprint on that filmstrip to nail your case down tight—"

Lauren Speers moved. Before anybody could stop her she charged over to where Craig was and slugged him in the face. Not a slap—a roundhouse shot with her closed fist. He staggered but didn't go down. She went after him, using some of the words she had used on me earlier, and hit him again and tried to kick him here and there. It took Orloff, the security guy, and one of the patrolmen to pull her off.

It was another couple of hours before they let me leave Xanadu. During that time Orloff and his men found all of the extortion money—$100,000 in cash—hidden in one of Craig's bureau drawers; they also found the red wig in the garbage can behind his cottage. That was enough, along with my testimony, for them to place him under arrest on suspicion of homicide. From the looks of him, they'd have a full confession an hour after he was booked.

Just before I left I served Lauren Speers with the papers Brister had given me. She took them all right; she said it was the least she could do after I had practically saved her life. She also took one of my business cards and promised she would send me a check "as an appreciation," but I doubted that she would. She was a lady too lost in alcohol and bitter memories, too involved in a quest for notoriety and revenge, to remember that sort of promise—running fast and going nowhere, as the comedian Fred Allen had once said, on a treadmill to oblivion.

I was too tired to want to drive all the way back to San Francisco, so I went up the coast as far as Big Sur and took a motel room for the night. I also bought myself a decent dinner in a place that overlooked the sea. Adam Brister would foot the bill for both as expense account items; I figured, after what had happened at Xanadu, that I was entitled.

Alone in my room, I tried to read one of the pulp magazines I keep in an overnight case with some toilet articles and a change of underwear, for motel stops such as this one. But I couldn't concentrate. I kept thinking about Bernice Dolan lying there dead and bloody on the cottage floor, and about what her neighbor in the Cow Hollow apartment building had told me of Bernice's passion for men and money. It was that passion, as much as Joe Craig, that had killed her. She had picked the wrong way to make herself rich, and the wrong man to share the wealth with. And the price she'd paid was as dear as they come.

I thought about Lauren Speers, too, and about Xanadu— the real one down the coast and the mythical one in the poem by Coleridge. "In Xanadu did Kubla Khan a stately pleasure-dome decree." Places of idyllic beauty, in both cases. The stuff of dreams.

But they were not the same. The dreams in the one I had just visited were of tinsel and plastic and pastel colors; of beauty measured by wealth, happiness by material possessions. Some people could find fulfillment with those dreams and in that place. Others, like Lauren Speers and Bernice Dolan, were not so fortunate.

For them, the pleasure domes of Xanadu were the stuff of nightmares.

ELEVEN

I got back to San Francisco at one o'clock on Thursday afternoon. The weather had turned cold and foggy; the Transamerica pyramid and the rest of the high-rise buildings downtown were wrapped in streamers of mist. The whole city looked insubstantial, almost surreal, as if it, too, were a mythical principality—the stuff of dreams.

I drove straight to Drumm Street, found a parking place not far from my building, and went in to find out if there had been any calls in my absence. There had been, a whole slew of them. The first four turned out to be anonymous; in each case the thirty seconds of tape following my recorded message on the answering machine were blank. The last five calls had been from Eberhardt, Charles Kayabalian, Kerry, and reporters I didn't know on both the *Chronicle* and the *Examiner.* None of them said what they wanted, just that I should get in touch right away; Kayabalian and Kerry both sounded grim.

Now what the hell was going on?

Kayabalian was the first one I called. He came on five seconds after I told his secretary who was on the line. "I was beginning to think you'd gone underground," he said. "Where have you been?"

"Down the coast on a business matter. I just got back. What's up?"

"Haven't you read the paper?"

"Which paper?"

"This morning's *Chronicle.*"

"No. Listen, Charles, what—"

"Go out and buy a copy," he said. "Read the story on page two. Then call me back."

Worried now, I hustled out and bought a *Chronicle* from one of the newspaper vending machines down the block. On the way back, I opened up the news section to page two. And then stopped in the middle of the sidewalk, with fog and people swirling around me, and started to shake with rage.

A three-column headline at the top of the page read: PRIVATE DETECTIVE ACCUSED IN BIZARRE HORN-BACK MURDER.

The news story underneath said that Mrs. Edna Hornback, wife of the deceased, believed I was to blame for her husband's death. She hadn't come right out and told the reporter that she thought I had actually committed the murder, but the inference was there. The inference was also there that I was suppressing knowledge of the whereabouts of the more than one hundred thousand dollars allegedly stolen by Hornback from their interior-design firm. Mrs. Hornback and her attorney, Ralph Jordan, were preparing a criminal-negligence suit against me, and she was quoted as saying, "I'm convinced a court trial will prove this man to be a menace to the people of San Francisco."

The rest of the story rehashed my account of Hornback's mysterious disappearance from Twin Peaks and the eventual discovery of his body in Golden Gate Park, and included a statement from Inspector Klein, who was in charge of the police investigation, to the effect that absolutely no evidence had been found linking me to the crime and that I was not under suspicion. There was also a summary of my involvement in what the reporter called "several sensationalistic homicide cases" in the past. The final paragraph allowed as how my record as a police officer and a private detective appeared to be exemplary, and that I had never before been accused of wrongdoing, but nobody was going to pay much attention to that. The damage had been done; I would look guilty as hell in too many cynical eyes.

I stormed back to the office, wadded up the paper, and hurled it at the wastebasket. Then, seething, I called Kayabalian back. "All right," I said, "I read the goddamn story."

"Take it easy," he said. "It's not quite as bad as it might seem."

"Isn't it? That crazy bitch might have put me out of business. Who's going to put their trust in me after a thing like this?"

"You're not guilty of anything illegal or unethical. We'll prove that. And we'll get a public retraction."

"By then it'll be too late."

"No, it won't. I've already begun preparing a countersuit for harassment and slander. I'll file it as soon as she and Jordan file theirs."

I said, "Why the hell did she go to the newspapers with this? I thought she wanted to give me an opportunity to prove my innocence to her."

"She changed her mind. Or her attorney changed it for her. I called Jordan as soon as I read the story; he said Mrs. Hornback tried to reach you several times yesterday, and when she couldn't she called the police. They told her you'd gone out of town on another case, so she decided you weren't interested in following her terms. That's when she went public with her accusations."

She must have talked to Klein, I thought; I'd told him, when I rang up the Hall before leaving yesterday morning, that I was going away to serve a subpoena for a client. Damn him. Damn *her.* I sat there with a stranglehold on the receiver and wished it was Mrs. Hornback's neck instead.

"What am I supposed to do now?" I asked. "Just sit back and wait and let her drag my name through the mud whenever she feels like it?"

"There's not much else you can do," Kayabalian said. "I warned Jordan he and his client were skating on thin ice; I think he knows that, and I think he'll keep her under wraps."

"What about the newspapers? I've got two calls from reporters on my answering machine already."

"Don't duck them. Prepare a statement denying Mrs. Hornback's charges and mentioning the countersuit. Stand on your record."

"Yeah," I said. "All right."

"And don't bad-mouth her or call her insane when you talk to the press. That wouldn't help your position any."

"All right."

"And whatever you do, don't contact her. From now on, under any circumstances, avoid her like the plague."

"Don't worry," I said. "As far as I'm concerned, she *is* the plague."

As soon as we rang off I called the Hall of Justice and asked for Eberhardt. But he was out somewhere on a case and wasn't expected back until late afternoon. I left a message for him that I would be in my office until five o'clock. Klein was off duty, but I got through to another inspector I knew; he said, predictably, that nothing new had turned up in the Hornback investigation.

My next call was to Bates and Carpenter. Kerry wasn't in, either. Still out to lunch, her secretary said. I restrained an impulse to ask if it was another business lunch with Jim

Carpenter; instead I left the same message for her that I had left for Eberhardt.

Calling the *Chronicle* and *Examiner* reporters was something I did not want to do, not yet; I would need to prepare a statement first. So I dialed Adam Brister's number. He was at his desk, and he listened attentively while I told him what had happened at Xanadu. After which he expressed the proper shock and dismay, but without any real sense of caring; the important thing to him was that the papers had been served on Lauren Speers and he stood to make a bundle out of her alleged negligence. He did express a professional curiosity in my own pending negligence suit—like everyone else in the city, no doubt, he had read the *Chronicle* story that morning—but it faded when I told him I already had legal representation. If he couldn't make a buck out of a given situation, he had no more than a superficial interest in it. Lawyers. He and Ralph Jordan would have made a good team.

I put a sheet of paper into my portable and began to type out my statement to the press. I was three sentences into it when the phone rang. George Hickox. And the first thing he said was, "Mr. Mollenhauer and I read about your . . . difficulties in the paper this morning."

Uh-oh, I thought, here it comes. The first backlash—the first alienated client.

I said, "Those charges are patently false, Mr. Hickox. I've never done anything illegal or unethical."

"I don't doubt that," he said. "Mr. Mollenhauer, however, expressed some misgivings. Not about your honesty; about the negative publicity."

I'll bet, I thought. "I see. And I suppose he's changed his mind about wanting me to guard his daughter's wedding gifts on Saturday."

"He did indicate that it might be prudent if another detective took your place, yes."

"All right. If that's the way he feels—"

"Nevertheless," Hickox said, "the job is still yours. I took it upon myself to speak up in your behalf."

"You did? Why?"

"You struck me as honest, reliable, and competent," he said. "And I've always thought it unfair for a man to be judged in the newspapers."

Hickox was the last person I would have expected to champion the cause of someone like me. Or, for that matter, to worry about whether or not a person was being judged in the newspapers. Maybe I had misjudged him; maybe underneath that stiff-necked exterior he was a decent sort after all.

I said, "I appreciate the vote of confidence, Mr. Hickox."

"Yes. Well, I also explained to Mr. Mollenhauer that it was a bit late to make arrangements with another detective. And that he and I and a few others in the immediate family were the only ones who would know you were on the premises; it's hardly likely that you'll run into any of the other guests."

I smiled a little, cynically. Now that was more in keeping with my original conception of the man. So much for Hickox as a sweet guy overflowing with the milk of human kindness. He was what he was. Hell, weren't we all?

"You and Mr. Mollenhauer won't regret your decision," I said. "I'll be there at two o'clock on Saturday, as promised—"

"One o'clock," he said.

"Pardon? I thought you told me it was two."

"I did. But the time of the wedding has been moved up an hour, to accommodate the minister, so you'll need to arrive by one. That's the main reason I called."

"One o'clock," I said. "Fine."

"Don't forget to wear a tux," he said.

"I won't."

The line went dead. I may have been given his vote of confidence, but I still didn't rate a good-bye. Common courtesy was not one of Hickox's long suits.

I finished typing up my statement for the press. It came out to a page and a half, double-spaced, and it sounded flat and defensive when I read it over; but it was the best I could do. Then I called the *Chronicle* and *Examiner* reporters and told each of them that I would be available for an interview at four o'clock. Both said they would be here and both sounded eager, like a couple of lions invited to a feast. Reporters, to my way of thinking, were in the same class as lawyers—feeders on the carrion of human misery. They may have been necessary creatures in the scheme of things, but that didn't mean I had to like them much.

I had had enough of telephones; I sat and worried. About Mrs. Hornback and her damned public accusations. And about the disappearance and murder of her husband. For the fifth or sixth time I went over the events of Monday night. No plausible explanation presented itself this time, either; the pieces just would not fit together. What was the motive behind the whole business? Why would Hornback's killer have taken the body away from Twin Peaks and dumped it later in Golden Gate Park? How could he have got it and himself out of the car without me noticing that something was going on?

The questions seemed to hang in my mind like spidersilk. I got up and made some coffee. I sat down and drank it. It got to be three-fifteen—and the telephone rang again.

Kerry. She had read the newspaper story, of course, and she was concerned; the concern made her voice .intimate, without any of the distance I had perceived in recent days, and that in turn buoyed my spirits a little. I told her all about Mrs. Hornback and how Kayabalian and I were handling the situation. Then I told her about the killing I had walked into in Xanadu. Talking to someone who really cared was a relief; my head felt much less cobwebby when I was done.

She said, "My God, you've really had a week, haven't you?"

"Yeah. Living my life to the fullest, that's me."

"I hate the detective business sometimes."

"Me too," I said.

"It's all going to resolve itself, isn't it? I mean, you're not going to be hurt by what that Hornback woman is claiming?"

"No, I'll be all right."

"Are you sure?"

"Positive," I lied. "Hey, are we still on for dinner tonight?"

"Of course. I'm going to bake some lasagna."

"Oh? I thought we were going out."

"Well, I've got a great lasagna recipe, and I thought I'd try it out on you."

"Sounds good to me. An intimate dinner at your apartment; I like that idea."

"I thought you would."

"And I'll bring dessert," I said.

"What did you have in mind?"

I told her what I had in mind. The only thing was, I said, I didn't think I could fit it into a cake box.

She laughed. "I swear, you're the horniest man I've ever known."

"It's a tradition among private eyes," I said. "Didn't you know?"

We settled on eight o'clock for dinner and then said our good-byes. I caught myself smiling a little as I replaced the handset. She was still my lady; the doubts and the jealousy I had been feeling were gone, or at least tucked away in a dusty corner of my mind where they belonged. The week had started with my love life looking rocky and business on the boom. Now it seemed to be the other way around. Never a dull moment in the saga of Lone Wolf, the last of the red-hot private snoops.

I made out a bill and an expense-account sheet to send to Adam Brister. I was finishing up the report that would go with it when the first of the reporters showed up, dragging a photographer with him. The other reporter and *his* photographer got there five minutes later. I handed out the statement I'd prepared and then let the photographers blind me with their camera flashes for twenty minutes while I fielded questions. The reporters kept trying to goad me into maligning Mrs. Hornback; I managed to restrain myself, keeping my responses polite and low-key as per Kayabalian's advice and my written statement. The four of them left at four-thirty looking mildly disappointed; the carrion I'd fed them had not tasted quite as good as they'd hoped.

At four forty-five Eberhardt called. He sounded less than sympathetic, even a little snottily superior—as if he found a certain small satisfaction in the predicament Mrs. Hornback had put me in. That sort of perversity was something new for him; maybe it was his way of fighting back at the world for the hurt Dana had caused him. But I still didn't like it much.

"I told you you'd find your tail in a sling one of these days," he said. "Welcome to hard times, hotshot."

"Yeah. But I'll get through, don't worry."

"I'm not worrying. But you should be."

"Meaning what?"

"Meaning just that. What are you going to do if your license is pulled?"

"My license isn't going to be pulled."

"Don't be too sure of that," he said. "We're getting some pressure along those lines already."

"What? From who?"

"The Hornback woman's lawyer, for one. A couple of others with some clout. The lady has a few friends around town, it seems."

"Jesus Christ, Eb . . ."

"They're clamoring for a suspension," he said, "at least until the suit comes to trial."

"You're not seriously considering that—"

"I'm not, but then I'm not the Chief and I'm not on the State Board of Licenses."

"But my record is clean, damn it!"

"That's the big factor on your side," he said. "It might be enough to let you keep your ticket. Then again, it might not be. We'll just have to see which way the wind blows in the next few days."

"And what are you doing, meanwhile?" I asked angrily. "You're supposed to be a friend. Why the hell didn't you put in a word on my behalf?"

"Maybe I did."

"Sure. I'll bet. What about your investigation? Haven't you turned up *any*thing in Hornback's background?"

"Not so far," he said. "He played it pretty close to the vest. Not even a whisper of a girl friend. No secret bank accounts or safe deposit boxes or large investments. The auditor Mrs. Hornback's got going over the firm's books claims to be able to prove shortages amounting to a hundred and eighteen thousand dollars, so it looks like she was right about that part of it. But that doesn't do you any good, does it?"

"Crap," I said. Which summed up everything I was feeling at the moment.

"You'll hear from me if anything comes up, hotshot," he said. "One way or another."

And that was the end of that.

The eased frame of mind Kerry's call had put me in was gone; a moody anger, laced with indignation, had hold of me now. I could not afford to have my license suspended. If that happened I would be out of business, twenty years of struggle and hard work down the drain. And then what the hell would I do? I was fifty-three years old; I had never been anything in my adult life except a cop; I was not qualified to do anything else. Get a job as a dishwasher or a ditchdigger or a delivery boy? Jesus. But I'd have to get some kind of job, because my meager savings wouldn't last me more than a couple of months. Either that, or start selling off my collection of pulp magazines . . .

No, I thought. Damn it, no. They're not going to pull my license; it won't happen. They've got no right to do a thing like that, no goddamn right!

I needed to get out of there, before I started breaking things. The one thing I wanted to break most was Mrs. Hornback's head, and that was a dangerous thought. I locked up the office and stalked to my car and drove home like a maniac, cursing other drivers, taking out some of my rage on them. There were no parking spaces near my flat; I put the car into a bus zone, the hell with it. When I came out later and found another ticket on the windshield I would tear it up and scatter the pieces. The hell with the city, too.

Inside my flat I popped a Schlitz and drank it in two swallows. Then I opened another one and went in and took a shower. The beer and the hot water washed away the last of my anger, leaving only the moodiness. Some day. Some frigging day.

And it got worse, too. I was just coming out of the bathroom, wearing my old terrycloth robe, when somebody knocked on the front door. I thought it was probably one of the other tenants, since visitors have to be buzzed in at the building entrance downstairs. My friend Litchak, the retired fire inspector who lived on the ground floor—maybe that was who it was. He was always after me to play checkers with him.

I went out and unlocked the door. But it wasn't Litchak; it wasn't anybody I expected or cared to see.

It was old Ivan the Terrible.

TWELVE

We stood there looking at each other. Ivan Wade was in his early sixties and so damned distinguished-looking he made me feel sloppy and rumpled, particularly now in my old terrycloth robe; he had brown hair and a neat black mustache—the contrast was part of his distinguished appearance—and a reserved sort of face with all the features grouped in close to the center. The first time I'd met him, my impression of his eyes had been that they were gentle; looking at them now, I decided that what they really were was cold. He wore a camel's-hair overcoat, a gray silk suit, and a perfectly knotted tie with a gold clip.

A good ten seconds went by in silence. At the end of it he said, "Do you mind if I come in?" in a voice so stiff he could have used it to punch a hole in the wall.

"I suppose not," I said. Which was a lie. I didn't want to talk to him, not now, all beleaguered and unprepared; I considered shutting the door in his handsome face. But then, maybe a confrontation with Wade wasn't such a bad idea. It was bound to happen sooner or later; it might as well be now—get it over and done with. I opened the door wider and stood aside, and he came in.

He had himself a look around. Dustballs under the furniture, clothing and magazines and dirty dishes strewn around —he didn't like any of that; distaste flickered in his eyes. The shelves of pulp magazines didn't seem to impress him much, either. Like his wife, Cybil, he had been a successful pulp writer back in the forties, specializing in fantasy/horror stories for *Weird Tales, Dime Mystery,* and other publications in the genre. But then he had gone on to radio scripting, the slick magazines, some TV work, and finally to novels and nonfiction books on occult and magic themes; he had even become a pretty adept amateur magician. He no doubt considered the pulps as having been something of a literary ghetto. Which made me, as a collector and aficionado, the rough equivalent of a slum landlord in his view.

He said, "You keep an untidy house."

"I like it that way. It's comfortable."

"To each his own."

"That's right. How did you get into the building? Pick the lock on the downstairs door?"

"I don't find that amusing," he said in his hole-punching voice. "One of your neighbors was just leaving; I told him I was here to see you, and he let me come in."

"Uh-huh. Well, to what do I owe the honor? I thought you were off selling books in New York."

"I was. Until this morning. I decided to fly back via San Francisco so I could see Kerry."

"Did you?"

"See her? Yes. I stopped by her office, and we had a drink together after she was through."

I could feel my fingers curling into fists; I straightened them out again. We were standing on my worn carpet, him near the couch, me near my favorite chair, with the cluttered coffee table off to one side like a barrier waiting to be slid into place. And we were going to keep on standing there that way. I was damned if I would ask him to sit down, or offer him any other form of hospitality.

I said, "So then you decided to come see me. Does Kerry know you're here?"

"No. I didn't tell her."

"That figures. All right, what do you want?"

"I should think that would be obvious."

"Maybe. But suppose you tell me anyway."

"I read your morning paper while I was waiting for Kerry," he said. "You've become notorious, it seems."

"That Hornback woman's charges are a crock."

"Are they?"

"You're damned right they are. Kerry knows that; she must have told you the same thing."

"So she did."

"But you don't believe it, right?"

"I have an open mind," Wade said, which was another crock. His mind was closed up as tight as a party politician's. "But the fact remains, you've been publicly accused and you're about to be sued for criminal negligence. You stand to lose your license, your apparent good name, and your livelihood."

"I'm not going to lose any of those things."

"Perhaps not. But the possibility does exist. And you must admit that no matter what happens, all this negative publicity will damage your professional status."

"I don't admit that," I said. "I don't have to admit anything to you."

The ghost of a smile, cold and waspish, turned one corner of his mouth. "That's standard procedure, isn't it? The invoking of the Fifth Amendment?"

I wanted to tell him to go screw himself. I wanted to stuff him into one of the drawers in the sideboard. Instead I jammed my hands into the pockets of my robe and glared at him.

"Assume your reputation has been irreparably damaged," he said. "Assume that whatever the legal outcome of this matter, you're forced out of the investigating business. How will you earn a decent living?"

"I don't think that's any of your concern."

"Of course it is. You want to marry my daughter. If she agrees, you'll not only become her burden but mine by extension."

"I don't intend to become anyone's burden!"

"How would you hold up your end of the marriage contract? Or would you expect Kerry to support you?"

"All right, Wade, that's enough." It came out hard and angry, like a threat. Maybe it *was* a threat. His icy control was starting to make me lose my own; I'm an emotional man and I don't react calmly to people like Ivan Wade. I could feel myself sliding into a dangerous frame of mind. "I don't like your insinuations and I don't much like you. What happens between Kerry and me is personal and private and I think you ought to stay the hell out of it."

"I have no intention of staying the hell out of it," he said. "Kerry is my daughter; I have every right to concern myself with her personal life. She made a serious mistake before; I don't want her to make another. I don't want her hurt."

"Neither do I. If she gets hurt it'll be on *your* head, not mine."

"Nonsense. You're not going to marry her, my friend."

"I'm not your friend," I said. "And I don't give a damn what you think or what you want. All I care about is what Kerry wants."

"She doesn't want you," he said.

"That's for her to say."

"And she will."

"I don't think so."

"I know so. She won't marry you."

A sense of suspicion, as icy as Wade's calm, began to slither through my mind. I could feel my face starting to flush, a vein pulsing on one temple. "You got to her, didn't you? Over that goddamn drink tonight. You bastard, you finally got to her."

"I do not like to be called names."

"No? Bastard. Meddling son of a bitch."

His own face got dark, like clouds piling up. He said, "You're coarse and boorish on top of everything else," and for the first time there was hard emotion in his voice. "I can't understand how Kerry could ever have been attracted to a man like you."

"I can't understand how she could have been fathered by a man like *you.*"

The clouds kept on piling up in his face. "My only consolation," he said, "is that you'll soon be out of both our lives. Very soon."

"Not if I have anything to say about it."

"But you don't. I told you that."

"I'll believe it when I hear it from Kerry."

"Then you'll believe it tonight."

"Is that what she told you? That she was going to send me packing tonight?"

"She didn't have to tell me. I know my daughter."

"You don't know your ass from your elbow."

"Crude," he said. "God, you're crude."

"That's right. I'm crude and I'm coarse and boorish, and I'm a fat scruffy fifty-three-year-old private detective. And you're a shit, Wade. You're the biggest shit I've ever laid eyes on."

"Damn you," he said. He had begun to shake. Which made two of us; I had been shaking for the past couple of minutes. "I believe those charges against you are true. I believe you're capable of anything."

"You want to see what I'm capable of? Hang around here another minute."

"Are you threatening me?"

"Yeah," I said, "I think I am."

"How dare you—"

"Get out of here, Wade."

"I'm not afraid of you, you know."

I took a step toward him. "Get out of here, I said. Or I'll throw you out. I'm not kidding."

He didn't move for five or six seconds; his eyes cut away at me like knives. But he was only saving face. He could tell by the way I looked that I was dead serious about heaving him out on his ass, and he was not about to get into anything physical with me; I had too much size and weight on him, and too much anger. He wheeled around finally and stalked out. He was not a door slammer; he shut the door quietly behind him, as if he felt by doing that he was getting in the last word.

I went into the kitchen and ripped the tab off a can of Schlitz and took the can into the living room and sat there drinking from it and shaking. It took a good five minutes for the shaking to stop and the anger inside me to ebb into a dull, hot glow. I quit thinking about Wade, but I couldn't quit thinking about Kerry. Jesus, what if he *had* got to her? What if she *was* going to send me packing tonight? I didn't know what I'd do, and that scared me. Too many things were happening in my life, too many pressures piling up; I just was not equipped to handle this kind of emotional overload.

When I finished the beer I took another shower, a cold one this time. Then I shaved and got dressed. I was strapping on my watch when the telephone bell went off. Even before I answered it, I knew that it had to be Kerry.

"I just talked to my father," she said. She sounded upset and angry. "What did you do to him?"

So the old bastard had gone right out and telephoned her. I should have known he'd do that; I should have called her myself, explained the flare-up to her before he could give her his own biased version of it.

"I didn't do anything to him," I said. "What did he say I did?"

"Called him vulgar names. Threatened him. For God's sake, what's the matter with you?"

"What's the matter with me? Listen, he showed up here uninvited and started in on me about the Hornback woman's accusations. Then he said he'd seen you and you weren't going to marry me. He seemed pretty damned positive."

"I didn't tell him that."

"Then where did he get the idea?"

"I don't know. He shouldn't have gone to see you, but that doesn't excuse your behavior."

"Maybe not, but he made me mad. I've had a rough day, I don't need that kind of aggravation."

"So you took it all out on him."

"No. It's his fault, not mine. Why do you automatically take his side?"

"He's my father," she said. "I don't like you threatening him or calling him names."

"You should have heard what he said to *me.*"

"Oh, God, I hate situations like this. Your side, his side —you're both driving me crazy."

"Kerry, look, I'm sorry if you're upset. But I'm upset, too. I don't know where I stand with you, and that's driving *me* crazy. Are you going to marry me or not?"

"I don't know yet."

"Are you sure?"

"Sure of what? That I don't know yet?" She made an exasperated noise. "God!"

"When will you know?"

"I don't know that either. I need time. Why won't you accept that?"

"Do you want me to shut up and go away for a while?"

"I want you to shut up. Stop pressuring me."

"All right, I'll shut up. But what about your father? Will *he* shut up?"

"I can handle my father," she said. "How many times do I have to tell you that? You just stay away from any more confrontations."

"Tell him the same thing," I said. "He's the one who came to see me, remember?"

There was one of those silences.

I said, "Kerry?"

"I'm still here."

"I'm sorry, okay? I won't let it happen again."

"Good. You'd better not."

"Do I still get to come over and eat lasagna?"

Pause. "I don't feel much like cooking," she said.

"We could go out somewhere. . . ."

"I don't think so. Not tonight."

"Tomorrow night?"

"Maybe. Call me at work."

"Sure. Fine."

"Now you sound petulant."

"I'm not petulant. Just disappointed."

"Me too," she said. "I'll tell my father you apologize for the way you acted. And I'll see to it that he apologizes to you, too."

Yippee, I thought. "I'll call you tomorrow."

"Okay. Good night."

"Good night."

Damn. Damn! I had been sitting on the bed; I got up and paced into the living room and looked out through the bay window. The fog was so thick that it turned the lights of the bay into indistinct smears in the distance. I moved over to the shelves of pulp magazines and looked at them for a while. Then I sat down and looked at the walls. I was beginning to feel claustrophobic.

I don't need this, I thought. I don't need to mope around here all by myself, watching the walls close in. I ought to go out and get roaring drunk, that's what I ought to do.

The more I thought about that, the better I liked the idea. It had been a long time since I'd got roaring drunk; maybe that was just what I did need. So I grabbed my coat, said to hell with everything, and went off to drown my sorrows.

I didn't drown my sorrows and I didn't get roaring drunk. I sat in a tavern on California Street, drank four beers, talked to nobody, developed a headache, and came home and went to bed cold sober.

It was one of those days you couldn't win for losing.

THIRTEEN

On Friday morning I got another jolt from the Fourth Estate. I bought a *Chronicle* on Drumm Street and took it into my office, and there, on page one this time, was a lousy photograph of my phiz that made me look mean and puffy, and a headline that said: PRIVATE EYE INVOLVED IN ANOTHER HOMICIDE.

It was the Xanadu thing, of course. The local press had got wind of it, as I should have realized they would, and the reporter had made a big deal out of what he called my "private eye pyrotechnics." The thrust of the piece was: Supercop or Shady Angle Player or some sort of Typhoid Mary who bungled into and out of disaster at every turn— which was I? The story was continued on the back page, where I found a second story, this one an account of yesterday's press interview and including the complete text of my written denial of Edna Hornback's charges. The reporter didn't draw any conclusions in either case, but then he didn't have to. All the sensationalism, and the lurid imaginations of the readership, would take care of that. No matter what anybody decided, I was going to come out on the short end.

But I didn't get angry this time; I was beyond anger today, wallowing in an oily sea of resignation and self-pity. I folded the paper, put it into the wastebasket. Then I made myself some coffee and sat down to finish my report to Adam Brister.

The telephone started to ring ten minutes later and kept on ringing at intervals over the next two hours. Kayabalian, full of sympathy and advice. My steak-eating pal on the *Examiner,* full of crap; he thought the whole thing was amusing. The manager of a credit firm I had done some work for in the past, whose duty it was to tell me, he said righteously, that for public relations reasons I would not be considered for future investigative services. Three media types, two from local TV stations, all of whom wanted interviews; I said no in each case, with more politeness than I felt. And, one right after another, two nuts—a young man who said I was a fascist pig and an old woman who said Satan had entered my body and my only hope for salvation was to embrace the Lord Jesus Christ.

Welcome to hard times, Eberhardt had said.

Yeah.

I finished the Brister report, put it into an envelope with the expense-account sheet, and licked a stamp. And the phone rang again. I was beginning to hate telephones; I was beginning to understand why subversive types went around bombing telephone installations. I picked up the receiver and said, "Satan Detective Agency," just for the hell of it.

"You're some guy," Eberhardt said. "If my ass was on the griddle, I wouldn't be half so comical."

"I wasn't being comical. You're the ninth person who's called this morning and I'm tired of it, that's all."

"You could get a lot more tired," he said, but there was none of the perverse satisfaction in his tone this morning. He actually sounded a little worried. "Things don't look good for you around here."

"Ah, Christ, what now?"

"The Chief wants to see you this afternoon."

"The Chief? What for?"

"What do you think for? I told you yesterday, we've been getting some pressure to yank your ticket. We're getting even more pressure today. He wants to talk to you personally, see what you've got to say for yourself."

"Yeah," I said. "And if he doesn't like it, he'll recommend suspension to the State Board. That the way it is?"

"That's about it."

"Terrific. What time am I supposed to come in?"

"Three-thirty."

"Will you be there?"

"Klein and me both. We're not exactly in his good graces, either; he wants action on the Hornback murder."

"Which means there still isn't any."

"A big fat zero," Eberhardt said. "Listen, if there's anything you didn't tell Klein about what happened up on Twin Peaks, you'd better trot it out for the Chief."

"I didn't hold anything back. Why would I?"

"I didn't mean that. I meant anything you might have overlooked, no matter how minor."

"Eb, I told Klein everything, down to the smallest detail. And I've been over it and over it in my mind since."

"Go over it again," he said. "Something went on while you were watching Hornback's car up there; you're the only one who knows what you saw or didn't see."

I sat looking at the phone after we rang off. It was going to ring again any minute; that was one thing I was sure of. And pretty soon somebody I didn't want to see was sure to come waltzing into the anteroom and set the little announcement bell over the door to tinkling. But I wouldn't be here to deal with any of that. I had a headache again and my head was full of enough bells as it was, like a groggy boxer in the late rounds of a losing fight; I needed air, movement, things to do. I switched on the answering machine, just in case somebody I did want to talk to called in, and got out of there.

The first place I drove was out to the Western Addition, to the house of a retired cop named Milo Petrie. Milo worked part-time as a guard and field operative for various detective agencies; I had used him myself in the past, and I knew him well enough from the old days to ask a favor. The favor I needed today was the loan of a handgun, so I could go armed to the Mollenhauer estate in Ross tomorrow. George Hickox hadn't been one of my morning callers, so I assumed I still had that job. And I still had both my license and a carry permit for a handgun; even if the Chief of Police decided to recommend suspension of my license, there wouldn't be any action taken until next week.

On the way to Milo's I reviewed the events of Monday night, everything from the moment I had first seen Lewis Hornback walking along Union Street. Restaurant, newsstand, drugstore, library, Dewey's Place, Twin Peaks Boulevard, and the lookout—all mundane, reasonable, without apparent significance. Hornback stopping the car, lighting a cigarette, sitting there in the dark, and my observation of the Dodge until the arrival of the two patrolmen—nothing in that, either. Still no ideas, not even any that I could stretch or manipulate into a possible explanation.

And yet, something Eberhardt had said kept noodling around in my mind: "You're the only one who knows what you saw or didn't see." That seemed meaningful, somehow, but I couldn't quite get a handle on it.

Milo was home, as he almost always was unless he had a job, and his usual talkative self. He wanted to know all about the Big Flap, as he called it; I suffered through fifteen minutes of explanations and a cup of bad coffee. But he was willing to loan me one of several handguns he owned—a .38 Police Special in a belt holster. He couldn't understand why

I didn't own a gun myself; I was an ex-cop and a private investigator and I had a permit, so why didn't I keep a piece around? I tried to tell him that I didn't care for the things much anymore, but that got his back up; he said, "Don't tell me you're turning into one of those antigun nuts?" I didn't want to get into that with him, and I kept my mouth shut through the rest of his firearms lecture. Then I thanked him, said I'd return the .38 on Sunday, and took it out and locked it inside the glove compartment.

You're the only one who knows what you saw or didn't see.

I drove back downtown. The place where I had made arrangements to rent the tuxedo was near Civic Center; I parked a half-block from the main library and walked over to the shop and wrote out a check to cover the rental fee and deposit. The proprietor insisted I try the tux on, to make sure it was a proper fit, and I let him talk me into it. When I looked at myself in the mirror, all decked out in the monkey suit, I thought I looked like a fat fool. My beer belly bulged and my shoulders bulged and my rear end bulged; I had never felt lumpier in my life.

What I saw. And what I didn't see.

I took the tuxedo in its carry bag back to my car and laid it across the rear seat. When I straightened up and shut the door I was looking over at the gray Corinthian-style bulk of the library. Something turned over, clickety-click, in the back of my mind. I kept on standing there, staring at the building.

Several things I *did* see.

And two things I didn't see that I *should* have seen.

And the library.

Sure, hell yes—the library.

Well, what do you know? I thought, and I could feel myself grinning humorlessly. The old private-eye pyrotechnics come through again. Just in the nick of time.

If I was right, my ass might be about to depart the griddle.

The Russian Hill branch of the public library was on Leavenworth, just up from the rowdy gay neighborhood of Polk Gulch. I parked illegally a block away—I seemed to be accumulating parking tickets these days, but I wasn't going to mind paying this one—and walked uphill to the turn-of-the-century building that housed the branch.

Inside, a middle-aged fat woman with glasses on a silver chain was holding forth behind the main desk. A youngish blonde, busty and moderately attractive, moved among the stacks to one side, reshelving books from a metal cart; I didn't see any other employees around. A number of patrons were in attendance, though—half a dozen seated at the reading tables scattered throughout, a couple at the New Books shelf, a girl using the photocopy machine, a guy loading up on paperbacks from a nearby rack.

My footsteps echoed as I crossed to where the fat woman sat behind the desk; except for the whir of the copy machine, the usual reverential library hush prevailed. The fat woman glanced up when I cleared my throat, put on her glasses, put on a smile, and said, "May I help you?"

"Yes, you may. A friend of mine was in here on Monday night and spoke to a young lady about a book she recommended. That young lady over there, maybe"—I gestured toward the stacks—"if she was working on Monday evening."

"She was, yes."

"Well, I want to ask her about the book myself," I said. "My friend told me her name but I've forgotten it."

"Miss Weeks."

"That's right, Miss Weeks. Jean Weeks, isn't it?"

"No. Her first name is Carolyn."

"Carolyn—sure. Was she the only employee here on Monday night?"

"No. Mr. Benson was on that night as well."

I was not interested in anybody named Mr. Benson. I said, "Thanks very much," gave her a bright smile, and made my way over to where the blonde was restacking books.

She was about thirty, hard of eye and thin of mouth, wearing a blouse that showed off her chest and a skirt that showed off her hips. She was also nervous and preoccupied; the section she was in was Archaeology, and the book she was shelving when I came up was called *Nude Photography*.

I said, "Excuse me. You're Miss Weeks? Carolyn Weeks?"

She gave me a startled look. Then she blinked a couple of times, wet her lips, and said warily, "Yes?"

"I'd like to talk to you," I said. "About the murder of Lewis Hornback."

I was after a reaction and I got one, all right. Fear crawled into her expression; she went rigid. "I . . . I don't know what you're talking about."

"Sure you do. You were Hornback's girl friend, weren't you? Among other things?"

I wasn't prepared for what happened next. I thought she'd offer another denial, after which I intended to tell her the police wanted to see her and then go call Eberhardt on the library phone. But she must have believed I was a cop myself. The fear in her eyes turned wild. And she threw herself at me, jabbed her elbow into my protruding belly, kicked me in the shin, and ran.

The blows staggered me, pitched me off balance into the left-hand stack; books spilled out and thumped on the floor. I caromed off, clawing at the shelf, dislodging more books, and my backside smacked the cart and sent it skittering away at an angle. Then I thumped to the floor, too—so hard that the rest of my breath came out in a whistling grunt. Book spines cracked under my weight; the hard edge of one bit into my hip, made me flop over on my side and bang my head against another shelf.

The rest of the people in there were on their feet making disturbed noises, half of them gawking at me as I scrambled up and half of them gawking at the front entrance doors where Carolyn Weeks was about to plunge through. I sucked in air, used it to say something obscene, and went lumbering after her.

She was gone by the time I dodged around one of the tables. Halfway to the door, a determined-looking guy in a brown sweater tried to grab me; I shoved him out of the way. The fat woman was shouting, "What did you do to her? What did you do to her?" in a voice like a fire siren. The determined guy came after me again and hit me over the ear with enough force to set up a ringing in my head. I brushed him away a second time, and by then I had regained enough presence of mind to yell, "This is police business! You understand? Police business!"

That gave them pause; the fat woman stopped shrieking and the determined guy quit being determined, and I got to the entrance without any more interference. I banged the door open with my shoulder, stumbled down the steps, looked both ways along Leavenworth.

Carolyn Weeks was nowhere in sight.

I stood in the middle of the sidewalk, panting, hurting in several different places. Three or four people were staring at me. I let them stare for ten seconds or so; then I said, "Shit," to no one in particular and went back into the library to call the police.

FOURTEEN

Eberhardt said, "You're an idiot, you know that?"

We were sitting in his too-hot office at the Hall of Justice, drinking coffee; it was almost three o'clock. His eyes were meeting mine today, but that may have been because he was miffed. I was not very happy, either. I had a bruise on my hip, a boxed ear, and a headache. Eberhardt had a headache, too, he'd informed me—and I was the cuase of it.

"Yeah," I said.

"All you had to do when you had your brainstorm was call us. But no, you had to go running over to the library yourself."

"I wanted to get a name for you. I wanted to make sure I was on the right track."

"Uh-huh. Well, you were on the right track, all right, but you went and derailed yourself. We'd have Carolyn Weeks in custody right now if you had the sense Christ gave a peanut."

"You'll find her, Eb. She won't get far."

"You'd better hope not." He looked at his watch. "Thirty-five minutes before we go upstairs and talk to the Chief. If Klein doesn't call in by then, your tail is back in the sling —but good."

Klein and another inspector, Jack Logan, were out hunting for Carolyn Weeks. The fat woman at the library had supplied her address—an apartment building on Arguello—and we'd all figured that was where she'd go from Russian Hill; it was the most likely place for her to have Hornback's money stashed. Eberhardt had put out an APB on her as soon as I called him, and the first patrol units had arrived at her building within fifteen minutes. But she hadn't shown up, not yet. Either the money was somewhere else, or she was too scared to go after it at the apartment. A search warrant had already been issued; getting that and tossing Weeks's apartment were part of what Klein and Logan had been sent to do.

I said, "I turned her up, didn't I? I figured out the disappearance and the murder. That ought to count for plenty."

"Maybe it does, in my book. The Chief might have other ideas. Not to mention the media."

He opened up a drawer in his desk and came out with a carved monstrosity of a pipe: the bowl was full of curlicues and shaped like a head with the top of its skull cut off, and the face in front wore a cherubic leer. He began to tamp tobacco into it. While he was doing that I got up and yanked the plug on his portable heater.

When I sat down again he said irritably, "What did you do that for?"

"It's too hot in here."

"If you think it's hot in here, wait until you sit down in the Chief's office."

"Stop ragging me, okay? I know I screwed up."

He made a disgusted noise, set fire to his tobacco, and blew smoke at me across the desk. That hideous pipe stuck in one corner of his mouth gave him a ghoulish look, as if he were smoking somebody's shrunken and lacquered head.

"All right," he said, "you want to explain this brainstorm of yours now or wait until we go upstairs?"

"I'd better give it to you first. I want to make sure I've got all the details straight."

"Fine. So how did you tumble to the librarian?"

"I'll get to that later," I said. "Let me ask you a few questions first, so I can lay out Hornback's disappearance."

"Go ahead."

"Did you see the body when it was brought in?"

"No."

"But you read the coroner's report."

"Sure I read it. Why?"

"Were there any marks on the body beside the stab wound and the scratches? Any other sort of wound, no matter how small?"

He thought about that. "No. Except for a Band-Aid on one of his fingers, if that matters."

"You bet it does," I said. "In Klein's report, did he say whether or not the emergency brake on Hornback's car was set?"

"Not that I remember. What does that have to do with it?"

"Everything. If the brake wasn't set and the transmission lever was in neutral instead of park, then it all fits. Klein can verify that part of it when he gets back."

"I still don't see the point," Eberhardt said. "How do those things connect with Hornback's body disappearing from the car?"

"It *didn't* disappear from the car. That's the point."

He frowned at me. "Well?"

"The body was never inside it," I said. "Hornback wasn't murdered on the lookout; he was killed later, somewhere else."

"Then what about the blood on the front seat?"

"He put it there himself, purposely—by cutting his finger

with something sharp, like maybe a razor blade. That's the reason for the Band-Aid."

"Why would he do a crazy thing like that?"

"Because he was going to disappear."

"Come on, you're talking in riddles."

"No, I'm not. The Hornback woman was right about him stealing money from their firm, so he was wide open to criminal charges. And he knew better than anybody that she was the type who'd press charges. He had no intention of hanging around to face them; his plan from the beginning had to be to stockpile as much cash as he could, and when his wife began to tumble to what he was doing, to split with it. And with Carolyn Weeks along for company."

"Keep talking," Eberhardt said.

"But he didn't want to just hop a plane for somewhere," I went on. "That would have made him an obvious fugitive. So he worked out a clever gimmick—what he thought was a clever gimmick, anyway. He intended to vanish under mysterious circumstances, so it would look as though he'd met with foul play: abandon his car in an isolated spot, with blood all over the front seat. It's been tried before and it probably wouldn't have fooled anybody, but he had nothing to lose by trying it.

"Okay. This little disappearing act of his was in the works for Monday night, which is why he stopped at the drugstore in North Beach after dinner—to buy razor blades and Band-Aids. But something happened long before he headed up to Twin Peaks that altered the shape of his plan."

"What was that?"

"He spotted me," I said. "I guess I'm getting old and less careful on a tail job than I used to be. Either that, or he just tumbled to me by accident. I don't suppose it matters. The point is, he realized early on that he had a tail, and it wouldn't have taken much effort for him to figure out I was a detective hired by his wife to get the goods on him. That was when he shifted gears from a half-clever idea to a clever one. He'd go through with his disappearing act, all right, but he'd do it in front of a witness, and under a set of contrived circumstances that were really mysterious."

"It's a pretty good scenario so far," Eberhardt said. "But I'm still waiting to find out how he managed to vanish while you were sitting there watching his car."

"He didn't."

"There you go with riddles again."

"Follow me through. After he left the tavern, Dewey's Place—while he was stopped at the traffic light on Portola or while he was driving up Twin Peaks Boulevard—he used the razor blade to slice open his finger. He let blood drip on the seat and then bandaged the cut. That took care of part of the trick; the next part came when he reached the lookout.

"There's a screen of cypress trees along the back edge of the lookout, where you turn off the spur road. They create a blind spot for anybody still on Twin Peaks Boulevard, as I was at the time; I couldn't see all of the lookout until after I'd turned onto the spur. As soon as Hornback came into that blind spot, he jammed on his brakes and cut the headlights. I told Klein about that—seeing the brake lights flash through the trees and the headlights go dark. But when you think about it, it's a little odd that somebody would switch off his lights on a lookout like that, with a steep slope at the far end, *before* he stops his car."

Eberhardt said, "Now I'm beginning to see it."

"Sure. He hit the brakes hard enough to bring the Dodge almost but not quite to a full stop. At the same time he shoved the transmission into neutral and shut off the engine and opened the door; the bulb for the dome light was defective so he didn't have to worry about that. Then he slipped out, pushed the lock button down—a little added mystery

—closed the door again, and ran a few steps into the trees. Where there were enough heavy shadows to hide him and to conceal his escape from the area.

"Meanwhile, the car drifted forward nice and slow and came to a stop nose-up against the guardrail. I saw that much, but what I didn't see was the brake lights flash again. As they should have if Hornback was still inside the car and stopping it in the normal way."

"One thing. What about that match flare you saw after the car was stopped?"

"That was a nice touch. When the match flamed I naturally assumed it was Hornback lighting another cigarette. But afterward there was no sign of a glowing cigarette end in the darkness—that was the second thing I didn't see. What really happened is this. He'd fired a cigarette on his way up to the lookout; I noticed a match flare then, too. Before he left the car he put the smoldering butt in the ashtray, along with an unused match. When the hot ash burned down far enough it touched off the match. Simple as that."

Eberhardt made chewing sounds on the stem of his ghoulish pipe. "Okay," he said, "that takes care of the disappearance. Now explain the murder."

"Carolyn Weeks killed him; I think that's obvious now. He went straight to her after he slipped away from the lookout; I make it that she picked him up in her car. Either they had an argument or she'd been planning to knock him off all along for the money. You'll find that out when she's in custody. But she stuck the knife in him somewhere along the line and then dumped his body in the park."

He nodded. "Which leaves how you knew where to find her."

"Well, I followed Hornback around to a lot of places that night," I said. "Restaurant, drugstore, newsstand for a pack of cigarettes, Dewey's Place for a couple of fortifying drinks —all reasonable stops. But why did he go to the branch library? Why would a man plotting his own disappearance bother to return library books? It had to be that the books were just a cover. The real reason he went to the library was to tell someone who worked there, tell his girl friend, about me and what he was going to do and where to come pick him up."

Eberhardt started to say something, but the phone buzzed just then. He picked up, said, "Eberhardt," listened for a time, and then said, "Right, stay with it." He looked in my direction as he put the handset down. "That was Klein."

"Anything?"

"He and Logan just finished searching Carolyn Weeks's apartment," he said. "There's no sign of the money."

"Damn. And still no sign of Weeks, either, I suppose."

"No."

Two minutes later, while we were sitting in silence, each with our own thoughts, Charles Kayabalian showed up. I had called him from the library, after listening to Eberhardt yell at me, because I wanted legal representation while I argued my case with the Chief. He'd had an appointment but said he'd be at the Hall by three-thirty, and he was as good as his word. I spent five minutes alone with him, outlining the situation. Then he and Eberhardt and I took the elevator upstairs.

The session in the Chief's office lasted almost an hour. It was a good thing I'd had the foresight to request Kayabalian's presence; he didn't say anything during my recap of the Hornback mystery, but afterward he offered an eloquent defense of my reasons for going alone to the library and of my professional conduct in general, stressing my record as a police officer and as a private investigator. I let him do most of the talking in that vein; he did a far better job in my behalf than I could have. Even Eberhardt, in his grudging way, allowed as how I had assisted the Department on a number of occasions and was always cooperative and aboveboard in my dealings with them.

But the Chief wasn't convinced. The stern set of his face throughout told me that even before he launched into a speech about how much pressure he was getting from various sources, including the Mayor's office, and how all this sensational publicity was harmful to the police image. There would be even more pressure after today's events came out in the media, he said. It was a public relations matter, he said. A private detective wasn't supposed to go around involving himself in homicide cases, he said, particularly when he kept making the cops look bad by upstaging them. He admitted that I had more or less exonerated myself of any wrongdoing in the Hornback case, but, he said, that didn't necessarily mean he could allow me to keep on working as a private detective in the city of San Francisco. He had the matter under advisement and would make a decision "in a couple of days" as to whether or not he would recommend suspension of my license. Meanwhile, it would behoove me to keep a low profile and stay out of trouble. That was the word he used: "behoove."

When he finally threw us out of his office, and Eberhardt and Kayabalian and I were standing in the outer hall, I said, "It doesn't look good, does it?"

"I wouldn't say that," Kayabalian said in his optimistic way. Eberhardt just grunted.

"Nice irony," I said. "He wants to yank my license because I'm too good at what I do. I'm not supposed to solve crimes; I'm not supposed to prevent crimes. What the hell *am* I supposed to do?"

Eb said, "Stay out of trouble. It could still go your way."

Kayabalian nodded agreement. "Let me handle this.

You're not going to get railroaded out of a job because you devote your time and effort to upholding the law, not if I can help it."

Eberhardt grunted again.

I said, "Yeah. All right."

But I felt like a goddamn prisoner as we rode down in the elevator.

FIFTEEN

I had dinner with Kerry that night—the first time I'd seen her since Sunday.

It was six o'clock by the time I got home and I was afraid she'd made other plans for the evening, but she was in when I called, and over her anger at me. Or at least keeping it under wraps. When I told her what had happened during the day she was both sympathetic and irate at the way I was being treated. And she agreed to dinner without having to consider the idea, although she said she preferred to go out somewhere rather than cook for the two of us.

I picked her up at seven and we went to a seafood place on the Embarcadero that had a view of the bay and specialized in calamari dishes. She didn't say anything about Ivan the Terrible on the ride over, and I wasn't about to bring the subject up myself; our conversation, for the most part, was limited to the Hornback case and to my session with the Chief of Police.

She was wearing a green dress, cut low in the front, that did nice things for her figure and for her eyes; she looked terrific. Just being with her took away some of the gloom I'd been feeling since my visit to the Hall of Justice.

We ordered drinks and calamari salads, and ate sourdough French bread, and she told me to quit dropping crumbs in my lap and on the floor. I took that as a good sign. She was always after me about my manners and general appearance and demeanor, but in a constructive way—a caring, intimate way. It was that old feeling of intimacy that I craved more than anything else.

The salads came, and while we went to work on them there was one of those conversational lulls. When I glanced up from my plate she was holding her head in a way that accented the clean lines of her face; the coppery hair seemed to shimmer and ripple liquidly in the soft lighting. A wave of tenderness moved through me. And I said, "Did I ever tell you you're beautiful?"

"More than once," she said, smiling. "But then I've always thought your taste is suspect."

"Not mine. Yours, maybe."

"Mmm. I sometimes wonder."

"About what you see in me?"

"Not that. Just about you."

"What about me?"

"Who are you, really. What goes on inside that shaggy head of yours."

"You're what goes on inside my head."

"Yes, I know. But why?"

I leered at her. "You know why."

"I'm serious," she said.

"So am I."

"Just sex? All those romps in the hay?"

"Come on," I said. "You know I love you."

"But why? Is it because my parents were both pulp writers?"

This conversation was beginning to get away from me; I sensed it taking on a significance I didn't like. "Of course not. What kind of question is that?"

"The pulps mean a great deal to you," she said. "More than you realize, maybe. Would you be after me so hard if my folks were doctors or social workers?"

"Kerry, what are you saying? It's *you* I'm after, not your parents. Sure as hell not your father."

"Don't start in again about my father."

"I'm not starting in again. I'm only trying to—"

"Why is it so important to you that we get married? We've got a good thing going as it is."

"I'm old-fashioned, that's why," I said, and I couldn't keep the budding annoyance out of my voice. "Where I come from, people who love each other get married."

"I'm not so sure it has to be that way."

"No? You got married once, didn't you?"

"Yes, and it was a big mistake."

"So you think it might be a big mistake to marry me, too."

"I didn't say that."

"Or maybe you don't love me. Is that it?"

"I do, after my fashion."

"What does that mean?"

"It means I care for you, very much, but I don't know you. I don't know who you are."

"Sure, you do. I'm an open book."

"I thought so at first. Now . . ."

"Now what?"

"I keep finding out things," she said. "Jealousy; I never thought you'd be so jealous. Or so intense about our relationship. Or so bitter toward my father. Or so . . . well, so relentless."

"I'm not relentless."

"But you are. It's a kind of macho thing."

"Macho? Me?"

"You have a certain dominant-male attitude, yes. You've got to have things your way; otherwise they're just no good for you."

I put my fork down—harder than I'd intended, because a couple at the next table glanced over at us. "That's not true," I said.

"You meet a woman, decide she's what you want, and a few days later you're pressing for marriage. That's machismo. You don't seem to care what I want."

"I thought you wanted me."

"How could you think that? You don't know who I am; you don't know me any better than I know you. All you know is that I'm the daughter of two pulp writers. And you love the pulps, and boy, wouldn't it be great to wrap up all your passions in one neat little package."

"That's a lot of crap," I said.

"Is it? What attracted you to me in the first place?"

"You attracted me. You."

"Not my background? Not the fact that we met at a pulp convention?"

"Listen, you were the one who came on to me, remember? How come? Your mother wrote private eye stories; you told me you'd been fascinated by private eyes ever since you were a kid. So what attracted you to me, huh?"

"I don't deny it was your profession."

"Well, then?"

"But I don't get off on the idea of spending the rest of my life with a notorious private eye. It's not that important to

130

me, not in the long run where it counts."

"Are you saying I do get off on your background?"

"I don't know," she said. "I'm just trying to understand who you are, why you want me so much. I'm just trying to make up my mind what kind of future we'd have together."

"It sounds to me like you've already made up your mind."

"There you go with that macho stuff again. Why do you always have to jump to conclusions when things don't suit your way of thinking?"

I couldn't think of anything to say; words spluttered in my head like a lot of faulty Roman candles. People were looking at us; we'd been talking in louder tones than either of us had realized. The anger we'd been building up lay as heavy as smoke in the air between us, and we both seemed to become aware of it at the same time. Kerry averted her eyes, put them on her salad bowl. I picked up my fork again and sat there holding it trident-fashion, like a pathetic Neptune.

"I don't want to fight," she said in a low voice. "Please, let's just drop it."

"All right. Consider it dropped."

We finished eating in silence, Kerry picking at her food, me compulsively wolfing bread and salad and beer. I made a couple of overtures at small talk over coffee, but it was no good; she had her thoughts and I had mine, and we had stopped communicating for the time being. Maybe for good, I thought. I felt low and helpless and confused; I felt lousier than I had in the Hall of Justice, or at any time during this whole miserable week.

We said exactly ten words to each other on the ride up to Diamond Heights. "Do you want me to put on the heater?" I said, and she said, "Yes," and that was it. When we got to her building I walked with her to the door. Fog eddied around us, turning the street lamps and apartment lights into fuzzy smears in the darkness. It was damned cold, but no colder than it had grown between us.

I said, "I don't suppose I get to come in."

"I'd rather you didn't tonight."

"Or any other night?"

Silence. She was rummaging in her purse for her key.

"I'll be over in Ross most of tomorrow," I said. "The wedding-presents thing. But we can do something on Sunday—even go jogging again if you want."

"I don't think so. I'll be busy on Sunday."

"Doing what?"

"That's my business, isn't it?"

"Another date with Jim Carpenter?"

It just came out; I hadn't planned to say it. But she didn't respond. She just bent over and keyed open the door.

"Kerry, look, I'm sorry. . . ."

"So am I," she said. She straightened and kissed me on the cheek, sisterlike; her lips were very cold. "Take care tomorrow. Don't get into any more trouble."

"I won't. I'll call you, okay?"

"Good night," she said, and in she went, and the door clicked shut behind her.

I stood there for thirty seconds or so, shivering in the chill fog. Then I tucked my tail between my legs and went home to sleep in my lonely bed.

I was up at seven on Saturday morning, prowling around my flat like a caged bear. I still had a compulsive need for food; I ate two pastrami sandwiches, some leftover Kentucky Fried Chicken, an apple, and washed it all down with a quart of milk. When I was done I felt greasy and bloated and mean. If anybody had come around just then I would have jumped all over him, growling and biting.

Last night's restaurant scene kept replaying in my mind. None of what Kerry had said to me was true; I'd been through that particular psychoanalytical trip myself, not long after I met her, and I had rejected the implications. The pulps had been a central part of my life for three and a half decades, yes; I had always tried to emulate the pulp detectives I admired, yes. But I did not allow them to govern my emotions. I did not love Kerry because of her connection to those yellowing old magazines and the people who had written for them.

The macho thing—that was crap, too. I didn't need to have things my way in order to be happy; I did care about Kerry and her feelings and what she needed. I loved her, that was all. I wanted her, wanted the commitment, wanted a life together. It was true that I didn't know her and she didn't know me; but we were learning. That was what love was all about, wasn't it? Learning about each other, unveiling secrets, taking the good with the bad—cementing the bond. No one could ever really know another person, no matter how close you became or how long you were together. All you could do was learn as much as possible. And keep on learning.

I should have said all that to her last night, I thought, instead of getting upset and defensive. Then I thought: Tell her now. Call her and tell her, clear the air.

So I went to the phone and dialed her number—but she wasn't home. Eleven rings, no answer. Eight-fifteen on a Saturday morning and she was already gone. Out jogging, probably; she was as compulsive about jogging as I could be about eating. Or maybe she was out with—

No. Forget that. Forget Jim Carpenter. He isn't going to come between you and Kerry; the only one who's doing that is you, smart guy.

I rang up the Hall of Justice to find out if Carolyn Weeks and/or the missing Hornback money had been located. They hadn't. Neither Klein nor Eberhardt was in, but Klein's partner, Jack Logan, was there, and he filled me in. Weeks's car had been found abandoned in the Sunset District; a lab check on it had turned up traces of blood on the front seat that matched Hornback's AO type, which added weight to the case against her. They figured she had picked up the money at a neighborhood bank in the Sunset area—a check of the city banks had uncovered a safe deposit box in her name at a B of A branch on Noriega—and then taken public transportation. Whatever else she was, she was also fairly cunning. Either she was holed up someplace in the city or she had managed to elude police surveillance at the bus depot, the Southern Pacific commuter station, or the airport. She could even have picked up one of the Golden Gate Transit buses that serviced Marin and Sonoma counties to the north; they made street stops at several points within the city, before heading out of it across the Golden Gate Bridge.

In any case, it all amounted to one thing: my ass was still frying away on the griddle.

I went out for some air. I thought about buying a paper, decided I didn't want to know what the media had to say about yesterday's events, and walked around for a while in the fog. Then I came back and picked up my car and drove aimlessly around the city, just marking time.

At eleven o'clock I headed home again, where I got into my rented monkey suit, feeling like the idiot Eberhardt claimed I was. After which I collected Milo Petrie's .38 Police Special—I had brought it inside the flat for safekeeping—and put it into a small portfolio case, along with a couple of pulp magazines. Then I clumped downstairs again.

Litchak, the retired fire inspector, was just coming out of

his ground-floor apartment. He looked me up and down and said, "Well, ain't *you* something to see. Going to a wedding?"

"More or less," I growled.

"I never saw you dressed up like that before," he said. "You don't mind my saying so, you look a little lumpy."

"I feel a little lumpy."

"Grouchy, too. Not that I blame you. You're getting to be a real celebrity these days."

"Yeah."

"But it'll all work out for you. People like heroes, and that's what you are. An honest-to-Christ hero, even if you don't look like one. Or dress like one."

"Yeah." I started for the door.

"Jogging suit last Sunday and soup-and-fish today," Litchak said behind me. "My, my. Ain't you really something, now!"

SIXTEEN

There was fog in the city, and thick gray billows of it coming in through the Golden Gate, but when I got across the bridge the sky was clear and the sun was shining. Nice day over in Marin. For some people, anyway.

I kept imagining that occupants of other cars were staring at me as I drove; I felt like a guy in a gorilla suit in one of those slapstick comedies Mack Sennett used to make. Look at the funny man, daddy. Isn't he something? Yeah. Litchak had hit it right on the nose, in more ways than he knew. I was really something, all right.

It was a quarter past twelve when I took the Greenbrae Avenue exit off the freeway, and twenty of one when I rolled into the quiet, tree-shaded affluence of Ross. The directions George Hickox had given me were easy enough to follow; I arrived at Number Eighty Crestlawn Drive with six minutes to spare.

The Mollenhauer estate was pretty impressive, even by Ross standards. High stone walls surrounded it, topped with iron spikes and pieces of broken colored glass embedded in a layer of concrete. A pair of huge wrought-iron gates were closed across the entrance drive; inside them was an old-fashioned gatehouse and an old-fashioned gatekeeper to go with it. Beyond, the drive hooked up through an acre of bright green lawn dotted with black oaks to where an imposing Tudor-style house sat on higher ground.

The gatekeeper took my name, used a telephone in the gatehouse, and came back finally and swung the gates open for me. I drove inside. Off to the north I saw, as I neared the main house, a second building of the type that used to be called a carriage house. It was being painted, and there was a network of metal scaffolding, ropes, pulleys, and suction clamps along the near side wall; that wall was a fading cream color, but the front was a bright gleaming white—that much of the job had been finished in time for the wedding. The scaffolding looked as out of place in these surroundings as I felt.

In front of the main house the drive blended into a circular parking area with a fountain in the center of it. I put my car between a Mercedes and a Bentley—nice company—and took the .38 and its belt holster out of the portfolio case. When I had the thing fitted on under the left wing of the tux coat I caught up the portfolio and stepped out. There was nothing else in the case except the two pulp magazines. I thought it would be all right if I spent my guard duty reading while I watched over the wedding gifts, instead of just sitting like a lump and merely watching; hell, the way I felt I was going to read whether it was all right or not. But I didn't want to just walk in there with the magazines exposed in my hand. There was no point in advertising what Mr. Clyde Mollenhauer would no doubt consider my lack of breeding.

A uniformed maid answered the door chimes and admitted me. The interior of the house was opulent, furnished with taste and care, all in antiques. She ushered me through a couple of rooms and down a wide hallway. Halfway along was an open set of double mahogany doors; we went through them into a study lined with books and appointed with masculine-type antiques.

There were three men in the room, all of them wearing tuxedos and looking far more comfortable and proper in them than I did in mine. When the maid announced me the oldest of the trio detached himself from the other two and came over to introduce himself. Clyde Mollenhauer. He was in his late forties or early fifties, tall and trim, with an air of forcefulness about him. He had straight black hair, penetrating eyes the color of burnt umber, and a Hapsburg jaw that made his lower teeth prominent when he opened his mouth.

If he was a bigot or a snob, or if he still harbored reservations about my honesty and reliability, you couldn't tell it from outward appearances; he seemed courteous enough, and there was no trace of condescension or suspicion in his voice. But I was aware that he had not offered to shake hands with me.

He led me over to the other two. One was George Hickox, looking as stiff-necked and officious as he had in my office.

I asked him how he was, and he said he was fine, thank you. He didn't bother to ask how I was.

The third guy turned out to be Stephen Walker, Mollenhauer's imminent son-in-law. He was maybe twenty-five, handsome in a brittle, actorish way; his hair, a wavy dark brown, was so flawlessly cut and combed that it looked artificial. When Mollenhauer introduced us Walker gave me a brief nod and looked right through me. This one I was sure about—snob all the way, as young as he was.

A short awkward silence ensued. They were uncomfortable because of who and what I was; I was uncomfortable because of who and what they were. What do the rich and cloistered say to a big, lumpy Italian private detective whose ass was frying on a griddle? What does the pulp-reading private eye say to them?

There was only one thing I could think of, and I said it: "Have all the wedding gifts been delivered, Mr. Mollenhauer?"

"Yes. All except a special gift for my daughter from me. It should arrive at any moment."

"If you'll show me where they are—"

"Certainly." He looked at Hickox. "George, if the man from the jewelry store should come before I return, bring him to the gift room."

"Of course, Mr. Mollenhauer."

Mollenhauer took me back through the house, down another hallway, and finally into a long rear wing; neither of us spoke. The near half of the wing's outer wall was made of glass, and through it you could see a stadium-sized terrace with an L-shaped swimming pool at one end. Three women in maids' uniforms were busily setting up buffet and bar tables and arranging pieces of white wrought-iron garden furniture. It was going to be quite a party; there was even a dais for an orchestra.

We went all the way to the end of the wing, where a window in the back wall looked out past some shrubbery to more rolling lawn and more black oaks. Mollenhauer stopped in front of the last door on the left and unlocked it. He led me inside.

The room's normal function was probably that of a spare bedroom; now it was jammed, like a kid's dream of Christmas, with what had to be well over two hundred gaily wrapped packages of varying sizes and shapes. They were everywhere—along the walls, on the double bed, and on all the other furniture—but you could tell that they had been laid out by careful hands, to avoid possible damage. A small table had even been positioned near the foot of the bed to hold the tinier presents; the seven packages on it had been arranged in a row, three with pink bows and three with blue bows and one with a white bow in the middle. Cute.

The only entrance to the room was the door we had just come through. An open door on my left revealed an enclosed bathroom, and a pair of closed sliding doors adjacent figured to conceal a closet. In the back wall was a wide window that offered the same view as the one in the hallway.

I went over to the window first. It was catch-locked and also bolt-locked—as a general precaution against burglars, not just to protect the wedding presents, because the bolt was not new. From there I moved into the bathroom. A window in there, too, high up in the wall; it was also double-locked. I went back into the room and opened the sliding doors and looked inside the empty closet.

Mollenhauer watched me do all that without saying anything. But when I reclosed the closet doors he spoke for the first time since we had left the study. "I had my staff make certain the room was secure before any of the gifts were brought in."

"I have no doubt of that, sir," I said. "It's just that when I take on a job I like to be thorough."

He seemed to approve of that. "Do you have any questions?"

"Just one. Would you like me to stay in here the whole time or out in the hall?"

"The hall, I think. You can take a chair from the other guest bedroom across the way. It's rather overcrowded in here; you wouldn't be comfortable."

Uh-huh, I thought. He did not give much of a damn about my comfort. He wanted me out in the hall so he could lock the door again when he left me alone, in case I happened to have any larcenous ideas myself toward the presents. Maybe it was just another general precaution, but more likely it was the Hornback thing; he may not have been suspicious of my honesty—at least he hadn't pulled rank on Hickox and had me thrown off the job—but he still wasn't taking any chances.

There was movement out in the hall, and we both turned. The young bridegroom, Walker, appeared and came inside, followed by a short, wispy-looking guy about forty, wearing a pinstriped suit and carrying a small gift box with a fancy pink bow on top. Hickox was there, too; he came in last, which used up just about all the extra space in the room.

"This is Mr. Patton, sir," Hickox said to Mollenhauer. "From Grayson Jewelers."

Mollenhauer acknowledged the wispy guy with a nod. The bunch of us were standing so close together that I could smell the mouthwash on Walker's breath; he glanced at me as if he were smelling something on my breath as well and not liking it much. The hell with you, buster, I thought. I gave him the kind of smile Bogart used to give people in his movies and backed away to stand in the bathroom doorway.

Patton said, "Would you care to examine the ring?" He

140

had a voice like the squeak of a mouse.

"Yes," Mollenhauer said. "I would."

The wispy guy put the gift box down on the table and took off its lid. Tissue paper rustled as he reached inside. A moment later he came up with a little blue-velvet ring case, snapped it open, and handed it to Mollenhauer.

I had a glimpse of the ring it contained. A gold scrolled job with a patina of age, indicating that it was probably an heirloom, with a diamond mounted on it as big as a cherry. The diamond's facets caught the room light and reflected it dazzlingly. I didn't know much about precious stones, but a conservative estimate of that baby's worth had to be in the high five figures.

"Perfect," Mollenhauer said. "You've done an excellent job with the setting."

Patton beamed at him. "Thank you, sir."

"Carla will adore it, Clyde," Walker said. He sounded as if he adored it, too—it or what it was worth. "It belonged to your grandmother, didn't it?"

"Yes. Of course, the original stone was much smaller."

Of course, I thought.

Hickox said, "It's one-forty, Mr. Mollenhauer. Shouldn't we be getting started for the church?"

"Yes, you're right."

Mollenhauer closed the case; Hickox took it and returned it to the gift box for him. He arranged the tissue paper over it and then put the lid back on.

When the four of them turned from the table Mollenhauer looked at me and frowned; the frown said he had forgotten I was there—me and my big private eyes, taking in the tempting sight of that ring. He made an abrupt gesture for me to go out into the hallway. I went and stood against the far wall while he and the rest of them filed out.

Mollenhauer shut off the lights, locked the door, and

tested the knob a couple of times. Then he said to me, "The reception begins at four. You'll be on duty until approximately eight o'clock, when Mr. Walker and my daughter will begin opening their gifts on the terrace."

Hickox had already informed me of that. But I nodded and said, "Yes, sir."

"You're not to leave your post at any time," he said. "Is that clear?"

What if I have to go to the bathroom? I thought. This time I just nodded.

"Nor are you to fraternize with any of the guests who might happen back here. I expect you to be discreet."

"I understand."

He put his back to me; he had nothing more to say. For all the attention the other three paid me, I might have been a floor lamp. I did not even get a glance as Mollenhauer led them away.

SEVENTEEN

After they were gone I got a chair out of the second spare bedroom and placed it so I could watch the door to the gift room, the window in the rear wall, and the length of the hallway. Then I sat down and looked at nothing in particular. My mind drifted to Kerry, to Carolyn Weeks, to the injustice of my status with both the police and the media, back to Kerry again—and before long I was mired in another funk. Which was pointless; I could brood all afternoon and into next week, and none of it would get me anywhere.

I stood up and paced back and forth for a time. When I got tired of that I reapplied ample duff to chair and took one of the pulps out of the portfolio case—*Double Detective* for February 1938. I opened it on my lap and tried to read.

At first, my attention wandered. But then the silence and the boredom combined to ease me out of the troubled real world into the fictional ones in the pulp. The issue had some good stuff in it—stories by Cornell Woolrich and Judson Philips, a short novel by Norbert Davis—and pretty soon it had me occupied. Time passed, no longer so slowly or quite so unpleasantly. From time to time sounds drifted in from the terrace, and once I heard someone call out that the caterers had arrived; otherwise the wing was hushed. Nobody came to check up on me, and nobody came to steal the wedding gifts.

This was a nice easy job, all right, and after the upheaval of the first six days of this week, that was just what I needed. Stay out of trouble, Eberhardt and Kayabalian and the Chief of Police and Kerry had all said. Well, I was doing that. And getting paid good money just for spending a Saturday afternoon reading in a quiet place. Maybe it was an omen. Maybe my luck was finally starting to change for the better.

It was three-fifty, and I was about to get up for the third time to stretch my legs, when the wedding procession arrived from the church. A silent procession, without the usual blaring of horns; the rich people of Ross evidently felt themselves above that particular postnuptial custom. I didn't even know they were there until voices and laughter rose from the front of the house and the orchestra began playing on the terrace.

Hickox paid me a call as the reception party got under way, no doubt at Mollenhauer's instructions. He said, "Is

143

everything in order?" in his usual stiff tones.

"No problem."

He frowned at the pulp in my hands. "What's that?"

"An old pulp magazine."

"Gaudy thing. It looks like a comic book."

"Well, it's not. Detective short stories."

"Well," he said disapprovingly, "I don't think Mr. Mollenhauer would like the idea of you reading."

"Why not? I've got to do something with my time."

"You should be staying alert."

"I can stay a lot more alert reading than I can just sitting here," I said. "You wouldn't want me to go to sleep, would you?"

"I should hope not."

"Don't worry, I won't fall down on the job. How was the wedding?"

"A very nice ceremony," he said, and went away and left me alone again with my gaudy reading matter.

Out on the terrace the party was in full swing. But judging from the noise level, which was low, it was not exactly a boisterous affair. Even the orchestra played nothing but soft background music. I was glad I was in here and they were out there; not only would I have been out of place among them, I'd have been bored to tears.

At five-fifteen a maid surprised me with supper on a tray; nobody had said anything about feeding me, and I hadn't expected the consideration. It was stuff from the party buffet: canapés, half a dozen little sandwiches with the bread crust trimmed off, two kinds of salad, and coffee. I ate all of it. Not as good as deli food and beer, to my taste, but then maybe I *was* just a lowbrow.

I had finished reading *Double Detective* and had opened up a second pulp—a 1941 issue of *Dime Detective.* The lead novelette was another by Norbert Davis, this one about a hard-boiled but wacky private eye named Max Latin. I liked Davis's work a good deal; unlike most other pulp writers, he had a wild and irreverent sense of humor.

I was more or less engrossed in the story, almost to the end of it, when the glass shattered inside the gift room.

It was an explosive sound and it brought me to my feet in a convulsive jump. No, I thought, ah *no*! Confusion kept me standing in place for a second or two; the noise from the crash faded, but after-echoes seemed to linger in the hallway. Then, jerkily, I dropped the magazine, dragged the Police Special out of its holster, and lunged across to the gift-room door. I caught hold of the knob, threw my shoulder against the panel. The lock creaked but held fast.

Inside the room something clattered, and there was a series of clumping sounds.

I stepped back, raised my right foot, and for the second time in three days I slammed the sole of my shoe against a door latch and kicked it in. The lock screeched loose; the door wobbled open. I went in after it in a crouch, the gun extended in front of me.

The room and its adjoining bath were empty.

That made me blink. And what I saw scattered across the floor brought a dry metallic taste to my mouth, made the multiple admonition *Stay out of trouble* echo mockingly in my mind. Two of the white-bowed and three of the pink-bowed little packages from the table were on the floor; the lid was off the one that had contained Carla Mollenhauer's diamond ring, the tissue paper from inside spilled out. In the middle of the paper lay the blue-velvet ring case, popped open and resting at an angle that let me have a clear look inside.

As empty as the room. The ring was gone.

Straightening, I ran to the window in the rear wall. A gaping hole had been broken out of it; the frame was serrated with jagged shards of glass. I shoved my head through the opening. But there was nobody in the shrubbery outside, nobody on the shadow-dappled grounds between the wing and the carriage house or the estate's boundary walls.

What the *hell*—?

I pulled my head back in, spun around, and charged back into the hallway. The bolt-lock on the window there released easily, but the catch-lock was stuck; I wrenched at it, cursing, and managed to get it loose. Outside, a short man and a tall bejeweled woman had appeared from somewhere and were making a tentative approach across the lawn. When they saw me heave the sash upward, throw one leg out over the sill, both of them recoiled and began to back up, wearing frightened expressions. But it was not so much me they were reacting to, I realized, as the gun I still carried in my right hand.

I yelled, "It's all right, I'm a private guard," to keep them from panicking and shoved the .38 back into its holster; if I had been thinking clearly, I would not have come out here with it drawn. "Get Mr. Mollenhauer. Quick!"

I climbed the rest of the way out of the window, dropped down onto the lawn. There was a sudden tearing noise as I did that, and the whole damned crotch of the too-tight tuxedo pants split open. It froze me for a second; I pawed at my rear end, felt my underwear and one fat cheek hanging out through the rip. I started to swear again, feeling foolish and violently angry on top of everything else.

A cool breeze had come up; it iced the sweat on my forehead, blew cold against my exposed backside as I lumbered over to where I could look along the front of the wing and out toward the entrance drive. I had a clear view of the forty or fifty fancy cars which crowded the parking circle. No movement anywhere among them. And no movement anywhere else in the vicinity, either.

When I turned back the woman was gone and the short man was standing alone, gawking alternately at me and at the broken window. I snapped as I neared him, "Did you see anybody running away from here before I came out?"

"No. For God's sake, what—"

Before he could finish the sentence, Mollenhauer came rushing around the corner from the terrace; half a dozen other people trailed after him. He took one incredulous look at the window, another at me and my ripped pants, and demanded peremptorily, "What's happened here?"

"I'm not sure," I said.

"You're not *sure*?"

"No, sir. It all went down pretty fast—"

"The presents? Carla's ring?"

I made a frustrated gesture with one hand; the other one was behind me, holding the torn trouser cloth together. "I'm afraid the ring is gone."

"Gone? What do you mean, gone?"

"Stolen," I said. "Whoever smashed the window got away with it."

He glared at me with his eyes sparking and his own hands bunched up at his sides. "Damn you," he said and then said it again with even more feeling. "Damn you!"

I looked away from him, over at the window. He started yelling something about calling the police, but I was no longer paying attention to him; I was staring toward the window by then, at what lay spread across the lawn beneath it, and there was a bristling coldness on my body that had nothing to do with the night breeze.

Shards of glass—that was what lay on the lawn. Scattered outward away from the wall for two or three feet, glinting in the fading sunlight. In the confusion of the past several minutes I had not registered them, but now that I had I couldn't believe what I was seeing.

They should not have been there. They should have been on the floor inside the gift room, because if you break a window from outside, the broken glass will always fall inward. That the shards were on the lawn could mean only one thing, and that thing was impossible.

The window had been broken *from the inside.*

EIGHTEEN

It took the local police just about fifteen minutes to respond to Mollenhauer's summons. But those fifteen minutes were chaotic. Word of the theft spread among the assembled guests and broke up the party posthaste. A few of the people left, presumably to avoid the inconvenience of being detained by a lengthy police investigation; nobody made any effort to stop them, and I had neither the authority nor the inclination to try it myself. The rest milled around on the terrace or inside the house in nervous little groups.

I wanted to wait in or near the gift room, but Mollenhauer was not having any of that. He subjected me to a two-minute diatribe, all of it vicious. "You're an incompetent idiot," he said. And, "For all I know, those newspaper stories about you are true and you're nothing but a damned thief."

"I didn't have anything to do with what happened, Mr. Mollenhauer," I said.

"No? Then where is my daughter's ring?"

"I just don't know."

"How could you let it be stolen like this?"

"The gift-room door was locked," I told him. "If it had been left unlocked, I might have been able to get in there in time to prevent the theft."

"I doubt that," he said bitterly. "You're a miserable excuse for a detective, no matter what the circumstances."

Hickox was there and Mollenhauer started in on him. "I shouldn't have listened to you, George; I should have listened to my better instincts. This man should never have been allowed inside my house."

"I'm sorry, Mr. Mollenhauer—"

"Sorry?" Mollenhauer said. "Go tell Carla how sorry you are, see what she says. I won't forget your part in this, George. You can count on that."

There was more, but I quit listening to it; it was pointless to try to reason with a man like Mollenhauer when he was this upset. I went and did my waiting where he insisted I should, in his study.

A nice easy job. An omen that my luck was starting to change for the better. Jesus Christ!

I sat there alone in my ripped pants, still a little stunned, and wondered what I had done to offend the powers that be in the universe. It must have been something pretty terrible to warrant all that had been dumped on me in this crazy week. Three simple cases, and all three take bizarre twists and land me square in the middle of a pair of homicides and a jewel robbery. My relationship with Kerry starts to fall apart. A lunatic woman slanders me in the press and threatens a criminal-negligence suit. I make an error in judgment and let a murderess escape with $118,000 in stolen money. And it looks, now more than ever, as though my investigator's license is going to be suspended. It was like getting sprayed with shotgun pellets—a scattershot of incidents that kept peppering me no matter which way I turned.

What next? I thought. What else can go wrong?

While I was sitting there feeling sorry for myself, the door chimes sounded and the cops trooped in. Five minutes later, they got around to me. The guy who came in was a broad, chunky type with olive-green eyes and a mop of pewter-colored hair, dressed in plain clothes. He was also a slow-moving, slow-talking type; the impression you got was that he deliberated each movement and each word before going ahead with them. His name was Banducci, and his official title was lieutenant.

Apparently Mollenhauer had not bothered to give him my name; when I showed him the photostat of my license he said, "You a *paisan*?"

"Yes. Swiss-Italian."

"Uh-huh. My people were Romano." He shrugged, dismissing the subject of ancestries. And then a frown worked its way onto his face, and he peered at the photostat again. "Wait a minute," he said. "I thought your name looked familiar. You're the private detective who's been in all the San Francisco papers lately."

"Yeah, that's me."

"Well, well. And now here you are in Ross, mixed up in another criminal case. You do get around, don't you."

Like Typhoid Mary, I thought. The harbinger of trouble and adversity, that's me. I said, "It's been a hell of a week," which was pretty feeble.

"You're in a lot of hot water, seems like."

"Through no fault of my own. I've never done anything illegal or unethical—not in San Francisco or anywhere else, including this house."

"For your sake, I hope that's the truth." He paused. "Mr. Mollenhauer tells me you're armed."

I nodded. "I've got a carry permit for a handgun, if you want to see it."

"Maybe later. You mind checking your weapon with me for the time being?"

It was a procedure request and it did not have to mean anything. Or then again, maybe it meant I was more suspect in his eyes than he was letting on. I said, "Not at all," and pushed the tux coat back and took the .38 out of its holster —carefully, with my thumb and forefinger. I handed it to him butt first.

"Thanks," he said. He put the weapon into his coat pocket. "What happened to your pants?"

"I tore them climbing out through the window."

"After the robbery?"

"Yes."

"Okay," he said, "let's have your version of what took place here tonight."

I gave it to him.

"So you didn't see anybody after you broke into the gift room," he said when I was done. "Not inside and not outside on the grounds."

"No. Except for the man and woman I told you about."

"How long was it from the time you heard the glass break to the time you got the door kicked in?"

"Thirty seconds, maybe. Forty-five at the most."

One of his eyebrows went up. "That's not much time for somebody to come in through the window, grab the ring, go back out, and disappear."

"I know," I said. The time factor had been bothering me, too, along with the broken window and the location of the glass shards. "But that's how it was."

"Mm," Banducci said. His voice was noncommittal. "Suppose you wait here while we go over the gift room. I'll want to talk to you again after that."

"Fine."

He went out, and I sat down on an antique sofa and

wished that I could smoke a cigarette. I almost never had a craving for one anymore, but when I was a heavy smoker it was times like this, times of stress, that the need for tobacco had been the strongest. Funny how the mind works sometimes, how it regresses and dredges up old desires.

I sat in the empty room and fought the nicotine urge and tried not to think about what Eberhardt and the Chief of Police and the media would make out of this latest mess. Instead I tried to find some sense in the theft of Carla Mollenhauer's diamond ring. The facts as I knew them were muddy and damned improbable. How could the window have been broken from inside the gift room? How could the thief have got away with the ring in less than a minute? Questions without answers, at least for the moment. And questions which seemed to contradict my explanation of the facts.

Another twenty-five minutes crawled away, heavy with tension, before I had company again. This time it was another plainclothesman whose name I never did get. He stood just inside the doorway and crooked a hand at me. "Lieutenant Banducci wants to see you," he said.

I stood and went out with him, through the house and back into the rear wing. On the way we encountered Walker and a pretty dark-haired girl of about twenty—Mollenhauer's daughter, obviously, because she was still wearing her bridal gown. The girl paid no attention to me; her eyes were red-rimmed and her expression was tragic and remote. But Walker pinned me with a passing glare, a down-the-nose look full of loathing. If he had any decent qualities, that boy, they were well hidden. I wondered briefly if Carla Mollenhauer was anything like him, or if she had made a serious mistake she would one day regret.

Banducci was alone in the gift room, standing by the window and watching a couple of uniformed cops working

the grounds outside. The sun had gone down on the opposite side of the house and there were lengthening shadows
across the lawn; dusk was not far off. The cops out there
both carried flashlights.

As we came in, Banducci turned and then came over in
front of me. His movements were still ponderous, but there
was a hard edge now in his eyes and in the set of his mouth.

"Okay, *paisan,*" he said, and he put a different inflection
on the Italian word this time, almost accusing, as if he had
come to consider me a disgrace to our mutual heritage. "Let's
go over your story again."

I nodded and repeated it to him, carefully, omitting none
of the details. Nothing changed in his expression, but his
eyes seemed to darken, to take on an even harder edge. The
tension in me sharpened to anxiety. I didn't like the way
things were shaping up.

Banducci was silent for a time. Then he said deliberately,
"Must be at least two hundred packages in here, wouldn't
you say?"

"Yes."

"And all of them still gift-wrapped."

"I know what you're getting at," I said. "How did the thief
know which package contained the ring? And he had to
know, all right; the ring box was the only one opened."

"So how do you explain that?"

"An inside job," I said. "Has to be."

"Sure. An inside job. How many people saw the ring and
its gift box after it was delivered this afternoon?"

"Mollenhauer, his secretary, his son-in-law, and the guy
from the jewelry store."

"And you," Banducci said.

"Yes. And me."

"Which makes one of you five the probable guilty party."

"It adds up that way."

"But it wasn't you, right?"

"No. I told you what happened, all of it."

"The whole truth?"

"Yes."

"One of the other four, according to your story, broke in the window, came inside, opened the gift box and the ring case, took the ring, went back through the window, and got clear away."

I didn't say anything.

"And he did all of that in less than a minute. According to your story."

"Look, I know it sounds impossible—"

"It doesn't *sound* impossible; it *is* impossible." He motioned me over to the window. "Take a look at this hole," he said. "Jagged pieces all around the frame—top, bottom, and sides. You see any blood on those pieces? Bits of cloth or anything like that?"

"No."

"But a man is supposed to have gone through there not once but twice, over and through all those sharp edges of glass, without once cutting himself or tearing his clothing. You think that's possible?"

"No."

"No," he agreed. "Look at the floor under the window. What do you see?"

Here it comes, I thought. "Nothing," I said. "The broken glass is all outside on the lawn."

"Oh, you realized that, did you?"

"Yeah. Just after it happened."

"Then you also realize what it means: this window couldn't have been smashed from the outside, as you claim it was."

"I didn't claim it was smashed from outside," I said. "All

I know is that I heard the glass shatter, and that's all I reported to you."

"The fact is, it was broken from *inside* this room—a locked empty room by your own testimony. Now how do you account for that?"

"I can't account for it."

"I can," he said. "How does this sound? You saw that diamond ring today and figured what it was worth, and while you were sitting out in the hallway you worked up a little plan to steal it. You kicked in the door, grabbed the ring, and then broke the window yourself. From in here, forgetting until afterward where the broken glass would fall."

"I didn't do any of that."

"The evidence says you did."

"I don't care what the evidence says. Listen, go ahead and search me. Search my car."

"We'll do just that. But I doubt if we'll find the ring that way. You'd be too smart to have it on you or in your car."

"Then what the hell am I supposed to have done with it?"

"Stashed it somewhere on the grounds nearby. You had enough time. And it wouldn't have been too difficult for you to come back one of these nights, late, to pick it up."

I had to struggle to control a surge of anger. Letting it out would only make matters worse for me, by giving the confrontation between us a personal angle. Banducci was just a cop doing his job, interpreting the facts as he saw them— the same way I might have interpreted them myself if our roles were reversed. I couldn't blame him for the position I was in.

In level tones I said, "Call Lieutenant Eberhardt on the San Francisco force. He's known me for thirty years; he'll vouch for my honesty."

Banducci sighed. "References aren't going to help you much, *paisan*. Not with evidence like we've got here."

"I'm telling you, I did not steal that ring."

"Sure," he said. "That's about what they all say—right up to the time the gates close behind them at San Quentin."

NINETEEN

They did not take me straight to jail. I supposed Banducci, in his methodical way, wanted his men to finish combing the grounds first before he booked me; if they found the ring, to his way of thinking, it would solidify his case. But he did read me my rights from a Miranda card—I told him I would waive right of counsel for the time being, but that if he officially charged me with theft, I would not answer any more questions without my lawyer being present—and then had me searched and put under guard in another of the spare bedrooms. No handcuffs, but two patrolmen in there with me instead of just one.

Now I knew what else could go wrong in this crazy scatter-shot week. I could end up in jail facing a prison term for first-degree robbery. That was the last pellet in the week-long peppering, and the deadliest of all: it had lodged in a vital spot, and it threatened to wipe out my future completely.

I sat on the bed, fidgeting, and tried again to piece things together. If ever I needed to have a deductive inspiration, it was now. The way it looked, nobody could get me out of this particular bind except me.

But none of it seemed to make any more sense now than it had earlier. The window could not have been broken from the inside—not unless someone had been hiding in the room all afternoon, and that was a literal impossibility; I had checked it over thoroughly, and the five of us had left together. No one should have been able to come through those sharp edges of glass without leaving some sort of trace of his passage. No one should have been able to accomplish the theft and then escape in a span of thirty to forty-five seconds. And yet someone had to have been in the room; I had *heard* him in there, knocking packages to the floor, stealing the ring.

Impossible, all of it.

Except that it had happened, somehow and some way. There had to be a logical explanation.

One of the other four, I thought—Mollenhauer, Hickox, Walker, or Patton. But which one? None of them seemed a likely candidate, considering who and what they were; any of them could be clever enough to have planned out a caper of this complexity. It had not just been designed to net him the ring under mysterious circumstances—that much I felt sure of, now. It had been designed so that all the evidence would point straight at me.

A neat, tight little frame.

Mollenhauer, Hickox, Walker, or Patton . . .

Something began to nibble at the back of my mind. I shut my eyes and concentrated, visualizing the gift room as I had seen it after breaking in. Everything exactly as it had been when I was in there with the four of them at one-forty, except for the broken window and all the stuff scattered on the floor. Or was it? There seemed to be—

And all at once it came popping through—the difference,

the one fact that opened a crack in the frame. I sat motion-less, working with it, backtracking. Once I had part of it figured out I remembered something else, too, and worked with that until it all began to pull together.

Bingo.

I might have become a Typhoid Mary and I might have developed a penchant for screwing up in various ways and I might yet lose my investigator's license, but by God I *was* good at my job. I could figure things out with the best of them. All, that was, except how to keep my life and my career from falling apart in one week.

I stood up and looked at the two patrolmen. "I want to see Lieutenant Banducci."

"What for?" one of them said.

"I know how the theft was done and I know who stole the ring. Tell him that. Get him in here."

It took them a few seconds to make up their minds; they were thinking that maybe it was a trick. Then the one who had spoken drew his weapon, held it on me, and told the other guy to go ahead.

Banducci was there inside of three minutes. "So you know who and how, do you?" he said. The skepticism was plain in his voice.

I said, "Yes. I can't prove it, but I think you can."

"All right, let's hear it."

"Take me to the gift room first."

He took me there, the two patrolmen trailing behind. The items that had been on the floor had been picked up and put back on the table; the open gift box and the ring case carried the residue of fingerprint powder. Otherwise, nothing was changed.

"This better be good," Banducci said. "You're on your way to jail if it isn't."

"It's good." I went to the table. "How many of these little

packages were on the floor when you first examined the room?"

He frowned. "Four or five," he said. "Including the one the ring was in."

"Doesn't that strike you as odd? The thief knew which one contained the ring. Then why were the others knocked off the table?"

"He—or you—was in a hurry. They were knocked off accidentally."

I shook my head. "The table hasn't been moved from its original position, which means it wasn't bumped into. And even a man in a hurry wouldn't be likely to sweep off four other packages by accident, not when he already knew where the ring was. No, those packages were knocked to the floor as part of a deliberate plan."

"I don't see what you're leading up to—"

"You will." I pointed to the gifts on the table. "There are nine packages here—four with pink bows, counting the gift box for the ring, three with blue bows, and two with white bows."

"So?"

"There were *eight* packages, again counting the ring box, when the five of us were in this room at one-forty. And only *one* with a white bow."

Banducci's frown deepened into a scowl. "You sure about that?"

"Positive," I said. I picked up the two white-bowed presents. Only one of them had a card attached; I put that one down and shook the other. It was heavy and did not rattle. "If you open this one, I'm pretty sure it'll contain something cheap and not very suitable as a wedding gift."

He took it out of my hand, untied its ribbon, and removed the lid. A wad of tissue paper. And the kind of hard plastic paperweight you can buy in a dime store.

"Okay, *paisan,*" he said. "So far you've got my attention. If this package wasn't here before the robbery, then how did it get into the room?"

"It was thrown in through the broken window from outside."

"For what reason?"

"To knock the ring box and as many other packages as possible off the table. The ring box was the primary target. The thief wanted it to hit the floor so the lid would pop off and the velvet case would fall out. He couldn't have planned that the case would come open, too, but it worked in his favor when it did.

"The bogus gift was a pretty clever touch. You need to throw something into a roomful of presents, so you make up a weighted one of your own. Chances are it'll be overlooked, and when it's finally opened, it gets passed over as somebody's idea of a practical joke."

Banducci said, "But what's the sense in it? Why knock off the ring box and the other packages?"

"To make me think the thief had come into this room to steal the ring, when in fact he hadn't, and to make you think I was the one who was guilty. If nobody else could have done it, according to the manufactured evidence, it had to be me."

"Are you saying he somehow stole the ring from outside?"

"No," I said. "He stole the ring when all of us were in here at one-forty."

"Yeah? How did he do that?"

"Simple. He was the last person to touch the case, the one who put it back inside the gift box. When he did that, as he was covering the case with the tissue paper, he slipped it open and palmed the ring. None of us suspected anything like that and none of us watched him closely; it was easy for him."

"Easy for who? Who are we talking about here?"

"George Hickox. Mollenhauer's secretary."

Banducci did some ruminating.

I said, "That's why he went to bat for me when Mollenhauer read about my troubles in the newspaper and wanted to bring in another detective in my place. I thought that was out of character at the time, but I put it down to a streak of humanity. He must have figured that because I was already under suspicion as a shady operator, I'd make the perfect fall guy for his little scenario. He didn't want to have to find somebody else, with more stable credentials, at the last minute."

"Let's say I buy it so far," Banducci said. "There's still one fact you haven't accounted for."

"The broken window."

He nodded. "The window that was broken from the inside."

"It *wasn't* broken from the inside," I said. "It was broken from the outside."

"So that all the shards fell out on the lawn? You know that's impossible."

"No, it isn't. No more impossible than any of the rest of it. There's a way to do it."

"What way?"

"Do you know what a suction clamp is?"

"One of those bar gadgets with rubber cups on each end?"

"Right. They're used by house painters along with certain types of scaffolding, among other things, and they're pretty strong. Remember the movie *Topkapi*? It had guys lifting up a heavy glass case with just that kind of clamp."

"And you think Hickox broke the window with one."

"That's what I think. He moistened the rubber cups, shoved them against the windowpane, locked them in place, and then took hold of the bar and gave a hard rocking jerk or two; the glass is relatively thin and the window is wide and Hickox is a brawny man. So the window broke outward, the shards fell to the lawn, and the clamp pulled free. Then he threw the bogus gift at the table in here and ducked around the front corner. He was long gone by the time I got outside."

Banducci ruminated again.

I said, "My guess is that he got the clamp from the painters' scaffolding on the carriage house; maybe you noticed when you came in that that building's being painted. And he probably returned it there afterward. If you can find it, it might have some glass residue that your lab people can match to the window. It might even have Hickox's fingerprints."

"All right," he said, "it all sounds reasonable enough. I'll give you the benefit of the doubt." He turned to the two patrolmen, both of whom were standing just inside the door. "One of you go find George Hickox and bring him in here. Let's see what he has to say."

Hickox did not have much to say—not right then, anyway. He put on an indignant act, denied everything, and tried his damndest to lay the suspicion back on me. But he had grown more and more nervous as I explained again how the robbery was done, and he kept wiping beads of sweat off his face. Banducci could read the guilt on him as well as I could; he began to take the same hard line he had taken with me earlier.

The interrogation was still going on when one of the uniformed cops Banducci had dispatched to the carriage house came running in, bright-eyed with excitement. He had found a detached suction clamp, but that wasn't all he'd found and brought back with him. He had thought to stir around in the cans of paint and turpentine left by the painters, he told us, and in one of the turpentine tins—

The missing diamond ring.

You could almost see Hickox come apart then, the way Joe Craig had in Xanadu. And when Banducci instructed the patrolman to have both the clamp and the turpentine tin dusted for fingerprints, Hickox broke down completely and admitted it. He had planned the robbery for days, even before making me his random selection as the fall guy—he had suggested to Mollenhauer a detective be hired in the first place—but he'd been having second thoughts about going through with it until Edna Hornback made her public charges against me; that had cemented his resolve. His statement as to why he'd decided to commit robbery amounted to two sentences: "I didn't want to keep on being a rich man's secretary. I wanted just a little of what Mollenhauer has for myself."

They put him in handcuffs and took him away. I got to go away, too, with an apology and even an expression of thanks from Banducci. I wanted to leave quietly, without any more contact with Mollenhauer and his family; there was nothing I cared to say to any of them. But on the way out to my car, I ran into the lord of the manor himself.

No apology or expression of thanks from him, not that I had expected any. Just a frozen-faced look and a curt nod. I would have gone right on by him without speaking, but it occurred to me that while I was in his presence I might as well tell him that I wanted just a little of what he had, too —my fee for the job I had been hired to do. I said as much to him, politely, adding that I would send him a bill sometime next week.

He said, "Go ahead, but I have no intention of paying it."

"What?"

"I owe you nothing. If you'd been on your toes, none of this would have happened. As it is, my daughter's wedding has been ruined and the family subjected to an ugly public scandal."

"You can't blame me for that—"

"I can and I do," Mollenhauer said. "Now get off my property before I have you forcibly removed."

I got off his goddamn property. Telling myself as I did so: You'd better stay clear of the heavy-sugar crowd from now on. You can't cope with them; they'll find a way to stick it to you every time. You common, screwed-up, ethnic private eye, you.

TWENTY

Sunday again. A new day, a new week.

I slept until ten, drove down to the foot of Van Ness and watched the bocce players for a while, then came back home and called Kerry. No answer. I opened a beer, turned on the TV, something I seldom do, and tried to watch a movie. None of it made any sense, like my life these days, but at least it was a source of sound and movement in the empty flat.

Eberhardt called at one o'clock. "You crazy bastard," he said, "you're all over the papers again today."

"I don't want to hear about it. I don't give a damn anymore what the media is saying about me."

"What is it with you lately? Why can't you stay out of trouble?"

"You think I plan these things? They just happen, that's all."

"Yeah. Much too often."

"Look, I'm in no mood for another lecture, if that's why you called."

"It's not why I called," he said. "I've got some news for you. You're off the hook on Carolyn Weeks, at least."

"She's been found?"

"Up in Eureka yesterday. Highway patrolman stopped a woman on one-oh-one for driving erratically, and she turned out to be Weeks. She'd just bought the car off a dealer up there, and she wasn't used to the way it handled."

"What was she doing in Eureka?"

"Heading north. Seattle. She knows somebody who lives there, and she was planning to hole up for a while."

"Did she have the money?"

"In the car with her. A hundred and sixteen grand in a suitcase. She'd spent two thousand for the car."

"How did she get out of San Francisco?"

"Took a Golden Gate Transit bus to Santa Rosa and then hopped a Greyhound for Eureka."

"What about Hornback's murder?" I asked. "Did she confess?"

"She did."

"Why did she kill him?"

"Stupid reason, like most motives behind crimes of passion. Hornback wanted to go to South America, she wanted to stay here in the States. They had an argument about it on the way to her apartment, the argument turned nasty, she stopped her car in the park so they could thrash it out.

Hornback ended up slapping her, and she grabbed a butcher knife out of a picnic basket in the backseat. They'd gone on a picnic on Sunday, that was why the basket and the knife were in the car. Screwy, the way things happen sometimes."

"Yeah," I said bitterly. "Screwy."

"So she stuck the knife in him and then dumped the body. She was too scared and upset to do much of anything the next few days; just wandered around in a daze, she said. She was just making up her mind to get the money out of the safe deposit box—it was Hornback's idea to stash it in there under her name, to cover himself—and split for Seattle when you showed up at the library."

"Has Mrs. Hornback been told about all this?"

"Sure. Klein notified her."

"And?"

"She's happy as a clam. All she cares about is the money."

"Did she say anything about me?"

"Not a word."

"So now what happens? Officially, I mean?"

"Your guess is as good as mine. I'm off today; so is the Chief. But I'll tell you this: he's not going to be happy about your involvement in that Ross fiasco yesterday. Or about the big media play this morning. They're calling you Super-sleuth. One of the columnists even suggested the city hire you and fire all the rest of us. Who needs cops, he said, when we've got Sam Spade and Sherlock Holmes all wrapped up in one package, rushing around solving crimes in a ripped tuxedo with his ass hanging out."

"Jesus," I said. "Was that in the papers, too? About the tuxedo pants being ripped?"

"It was. They played it for laughs."

I could feel an angry flush coming up out of my collar; I wanted to hit something. Instead I said, "That ought to put me in solid with everybody."

"I warned you, hotshot."

"Sure. You warned me."

"Listen," he said, "I'd invite you over for a beer, but I don't think you'd be very good company. Neither would I, for that matter. Just hang in there, okay? I'll be in touch as soon as I hear anything from the Chief's office."

After he rang off I called Kerry again. Still no answer. The TV was still blaring away; I went out and shut it off and then opened another beer, but I didn't want that either. About the only activity that appealed to me was a long drive, so I took my car all the way out to the Point Reyes lighthouse, through gray mist and rugged terrain that matched my mood. It was after nine o'clock when I got back, tired and crabby and dull-witted. I tried Kerry once more, but she still wasn't in. Which left nothing to do except to crawl into bed.

End of Sunday. Beginning of the end.

On Monday morning I took what was left of the rented tuxedo back to its owner. He refused to refund my deposit; the trousers were ruined, he said; he couldn't mend them; it was people like me who made things difficult for everyone. There was no arguing with that on any level; I didn't even try.

When I got to my office there were all sorts of messages on my answering machine, mostly from media people. I didn't return any of the calls. And I left the machine on so I wouldn't have to deal with any of the other calls that came in. I also went out and locked the outer door; I didn't want to be bothered by visitors, either.

I made out a bill to Clyde Mollenhauer and put it into an envelope with a copy of the contract Hickox had signed as his agent and a short and not very polite note threatening to take him to small-claims court if he didn't pay up. After which I did the same thing for Edna Hornback; no matter what she intended to do now, she owed me money and I was going to collect it one way or another.

Later in the morning I called Kayabalian. "I've been trying to reach you," he said, "but I kept getting your answering machine."

"I'm not taking calls this morning."

"You've heard about the arrest of Carolyn Weeks?"

"I've heard."

"Well, I've been in touch with Ralph Jordan, Mrs. Hornback's attorney. They're dropping their plans for a criminal-negligence suit."

"That's good news, I suppose."

"Yes. I warned him we might go ahead with a slander and harassment suit against his client, but he said if we did that, they'd reactivate their suit. I think it would be best if we backed off, too."

"Whatever you say."

"As for your situation with the police . . . well, that robbery you were involved in on Saturday isn't going to help you any."

"So I've been told."

"I wish that hadn't happened," he said. "We'd be on much firmer ground if you'd stayed clear of any more trouble."

I was tired of defending myself against that particular accusation; I didn't say anything.

"I'll plead your case again with the Chief of Police. There's a chance I can get him to listen to reason in spite of all the publicity."

"Sure. Do what you think is best."

"Don't give up hope," he said. "Call me again late this afternoon. I'll be here until five."

"All right."

I went out for a few minutes to mail my letters. When I came back it was eleven-thirty and Kerry was sitting on one of the chairs in the anteroom; I had forgotten to relock the door. "I just got here," she said. "Your door was open, so I thought I'd wait."

"Come into my office. I'll make us some coffee."

"No, I can't stay long. I've got a lunch at noon."

Her eyes were dark and grave, and there was something in them and in her voice that made me look away from her. I said, "I guess you read about the big doings over in Ross."

"Yes." She stood up, started to touch my arm and then withdrew her hand. "I'm sorry," she said.

"Me too."

"Have you heard anything more from the police? About whether they're going to let you keep your license?"

"Not yet. Maybe later today."

"Do you think they will?"

"I don't know. Kayabalian is going to plead my case to the Chief again. The Hornback woman is dropping her lawsuit; that's one point in my favor."

"Will you call me as soon as you hear?"

"If you want me to."

We were silent—one of those awkward, pregnant silences with unspoken things hanging in the air as heavy and gray as the fog outside. I faced her again; emotions churned inside me like half-raw meat stewing in the bottom of a pot.

I said, "You didn't just come here to offer me sympathy, did you?"

She shook her head. "No."

"You've made up your mind, right? And the answer is no."

"I haven't made up my mind. But I do think . . ." She broke off.

"What?"

"I know this is a bad time for you, but . . . I think it would be better if we didn't see each other for a while."

There was a thickness in my throat; I had to push words up through it. "How long a while?"

"A week or two."

Or three or four or forever, I thought. I looked away from her again.

"I need time," she said. "We both do. We're not any good for each other the way things are now."

I said nothing; I had nothing to say.

"It'll take the pressure off both of us," she said. "That way, we can both make a decision—how we feel, what we want."

"I know what I feel and what I want."

"I'm not so sure you do. And I know I don't. I need freedom to make a decision as important as this."

"Maybe you just need freedom," I said.

The skin along her left cheekbone rippled in what might have been a wince. "Maybe," she said. "And maybe not. I just don't know yet."

"Okay, then. We'll do it your way—any way you want. We won't see each other. I won't call you."

"You can call me if you need to talk about things."

"Things other than us, you mean."

"It's best that way, believe me. For now."

"Sure. For now."

"I'd better go," she said. "And please call when you hear about your license. Will you do that?"

"Yes."

She stayed a moment longer, looking at me with her grave chameleon eyes. Then she smiled a small smile and said, "Take care of yourself, for heaven's sake," and I watched her turn and walk out through the anteroom, through the outer door—away, gone. I kept on standing there, staring at the empty spaces where she'd been, all the empty spaces where she'd been.

Good-bye, Kerry, I thought.

I called Kayabalian at four-thirty, from my flat; I'd gone home early because there was nothing to do at the office and nowhere else to go. And he said, "I'm afraid I've got some bad news," in a voice as grave as Kerry's had been.

I waited.

"The Chief of Police has decided to recommend suspension to the State Board of Licenses. I tried to get him to change his mind, but he's in a snit over that Ross business and all the flap in the media; he won't budge."

"I see. An indefinite suspension?"

"Yes. There's still a chance the Board will reject the recommendation. Not much of a one, I've got to be honest with you, but it could happen. They'll probably schedule a hearing later in the week; I'll go with you, and we'll make one more try. If they do suspend your license, we can sue for reinstatement—but frankly, that's a long and expensive process."

"So there's not much I can do, is there?" I said. "Just let them take away my livelihood and go out and get another job and chalk it all up to experience. Grin and bear it."

"I'm sorry," Kayabalian said. "I really am sorry."

I thanked him for all he'd done and went out and stood in the bay window, watching the fog swirl and eddy and turn the whole world gray. Something had got into one of my eyes; I could feel wetness forming there. I brushed it away. So that's that, I thought. Not with a bang but a whimper—that's the way it ends. No business, no money, no

Kerry, no prospects. Where do I go from here? Where the hell do I go from here?

Welcome to hard times . . .